THE ROGUE'S REDEMPTION

CECELIA MECCA

To Leeta and Karla, Nosh book plotting and wine.
And not using the Oxford comma.

rockburg Castle, Scotland, 1273

Reid grew bold as the maid deepened their kiss. When his hand moved upward from her waist, her soft groan was all the encouragement he needed. Certain they could not be seen, hidden in a small alcove at the foot of a rarely used staircase, he explored the curves that had taunted him since she'd arrived the week before. A new lady's maid at Brockburg, and just what he needed to forget about the selection.

"What is your name?" he thought to ask, breaking contact and watching as his hand reached its goal.

"Anne," said the pretty blonde.

He could think of nothing else to say that mattered, so he resumed the kiss. Dipping his fingers below the neckline of her very inconvenient gown, Reid finally managed to—

"Brother."

The unwelcome voice sounded annoyed. The maid pulled away.

Rather than turn toward the sound, he murmured, "Not now," and tried to resume what had been so rudely interrupted.

The maid, Anne, pushed his hand away and stood ramrod

straight. Their interlude was apparently at an end now that the chief had arrived.

Reid turned and watched as Anne nodded a quick bow and ran. Though it was difficult to fully see her backside from this vantage point—

"Christ, Reid. She's gone."

He sighed, not caring if Toren noticed. "I'll assume this is important?"

Toren didn't answer. Instead, he narrowed his eyes at Reid, eyes the same brown-green as his own.

There was judgment there. As usual.

Though he and his brother disagreed at times, they rarely fought as they had this morning. Apparently his brother was still displeased with him. Maybe even more so.

"There's been another raid."

That got his attention.

"When?" he asked as Toren turned and made his way up the stone staircase that led to the great hall. "Where?"

The maid completely forgotten, he followed Toren through the hall's entrance and then toward the front doors of the keep.

"No more than an hour past. On a farm near the southern border. English reivers. They took naught but cattle."

Raids, though common in the borderlands, rarely occurred on Kerr land. The Kerrs' reputation for being fierce warriors had spread widely enough to grant them a modicum of peace.

As they approached the stables, Reid caught the attention of a groom who had just exited the stone building.

"Prepare our horses," he shouted, and the groom immediately about-faced to do as he was bid. "Where are the other men?" he asked.

When a Hot Trod commenced, it typically included at least five or six clansmen. To ride out with less was a risk not worth taking.

"Already waiting beyond the gates," Toren said. "It took some time to find you."

He would not apologize, and Toren wouldn't expect him to. Instead, they stood in silence until the groom returned with their horses. The man had prepared them with admirable haste.

The brothers mounted and rode through the courtyard toward the gatehouse. Brockburg had just one defensive wall, but its compact design and high vantage which afforded views well beyond its gates, secured it well.

As they met up with the others, Toren looked straight at him. "We pursue but do not kill."

He nodded his acceptance, and they began to ride out.

Though he hoped Toren would leave their argument be, it wasn't long before his brother yelled out, "We still need to talk."

Luckily, their hasty pursuit south toward the border prohibited any further discussion. For now.

Damn Alex. This whole mess with Toren was his middle brother's fault for giving up his position. Reid liked Clara well enough, but if Alex had not married her and moved to Dunmure Tower, he and Toren would not have spent a good portion of the summer disagreeing about the future of their clan.

The elders would choose a second soon, and while Toren would have it be him, Reid was content as his brother's chief guard.

"Tracks," Toren yelled to the men, jarring him out of his thoughts. His brother was right. They were getting closer, and at this pace, the question was not whether they would catch up to the English bastards, but whether he could follow his brother's decree.

The tracks led them directly to a camp of five men who were very much reivers by the look of them. Oddly enough, there were no cattle in sight and the men they'd come upon did not even attempt to fight or flee. Instead, they allowed themselves to be surrounded by Toren and his men.

Something wasn't right.

The fools had not even bothered to cross the border into England before stopping. They were either the most inept reivers Reid had come across or too stupid to realize who they'd stolen from.

Reid had just ridden up beside his brother when one of the dismounted reivers rushed toward Toren, moving with astounding speed.

Reid barely realized he'd dismounted or drawn his dagger. He'd positioned himself between his brother and the reiver so quickly that none of the others had time to react. Toren's would-be attacker lifted his lang spear and positioned it directly in line to hit his brother. Reid tossed his dirk through the air, its aim true. The man howled in pain as the spear dropped from his hand. He threw his other hand into the air, blood beginning to seep through and color his sleeve red.

Reid grabbed the man near the top of his quilted gambeson and yanked his dirk from the man's arm.

"You threaten the life of the wrong man," he growled, pressing the blood-stained dagger to the man's throat. The reiver's life was in his hands now. If he said the wrong thing, Reid could not be responsible for his actions.

"'Twas foolish," he cried. "We were caught unaware."

Reid did not look to his brother for permission. He didn't glance at any of the other men, knowing he was protected. If the reivers moved, his clansmen would cut them down where they cowered.

"You stole from Clan Kerr," he said. "You threaten its chief."

The look in the man's eyes surprised him. He was entirely unafraid.

"You and your men will come with us to the warden."

The man offered neither a response nor an argument. The English bastard simply stared straight back at him as if daring him to do his worst.

Reid itched to do so.

"Enough," Toren called, deciding for him. His brother dismounted and plunged his hands into the saddlebag at his side. He knew precisely what Toren intended. The reivers would be bound and taken to James Douglas, Lord Warden of the Eastern Marches. They would be held until the next Day of Truce, whereupon judgment would be meted out for their crimes.

Reid turned the man around and allowed Toren and the others to begin the task of securing the prisoners.

"Where are the cattle?" he asked, and received glares rather than a response. He caught Toren's eye, his silent question answered by a shake of the head.

They would let Douglas question them.

One of Reid's men clapped him on the back, presumably for protecting his brother, but he could not join in his clansman's relief.

Something was amiss with these men, this raid, and he intended to find out what it was.

***

"Will you meet me later?" Allie Bowman asked her brother-in-law.

Aidan crossed his arms. He disliked keeping their training sessions private, but Allie had just escaped an unwanted betrothal, preceded by a lifetime of others making her decisions for her. She was owed this one secret.

"You are relentless," he said with a smile, a sure sign he was about to say yes. "It will be dark soon—"

"But not yet."

Allie looked up as if the sky would reveal how much time they had remaining. For the past three days the sun had refused to show itself, an indication, had they needed one, that a change of season was upon them. Soon warm days would be replaced with cool, autumn evenings.

"Your friend has returned."

She'd already felt the soft brush of fur through the fabric of her dress. The kitten seemed to have come from nowhere a few days earlier. No one was able to locate her parents. Allie wished to help her, but each time she reached down to scoop up her furry friend, the kitten ran away.

This time, Aidan stopped her as soon as she moved her hand.

"Let her get accustomed to you," he said. "She may not be ready just yet."

It was not Allie's nature to be patient, but she took his advice and simply watched the brown and gray kitten with her white paws and the adorable white patch on her face. When her restraint cracked and she reached down to pet the kitten, the little one ran away.

"I will meet you there as soon as I speak to Graeme." With that, Aidan winked and turned toward the keep.

Allie smiled to herself. She'd known he would come.

Rather than follow him into the keep, she leaned against the cold stone wall of Highgate Castle. Perhaps she should reconsider and tell her sister about the lessons. After all, Gillian was nothing like their parents, though she'd become a mite more protective now that Allie was living in Scotland.

As far as Allie was concerned, she was never, ever going back. After one near brush with marriage to a completely inappropriate and undesirable man, the Earl of Covington, she did not plan on allowing her father to arrange a match with another wealthy old bore. He was the last person in the borderlands she'd trust with her future. Still, he kept trying. Indeed, his latest attempt to lure her back to England had arrived the day before.

After changing into an outfit appropriate for training—tights and a loose linen shirt she'd borrowed from her brother-in-law— Allie spent the next hour visiting the armorer. When she finally spotted Aidan leaving the keep, Allie slowly followed. She took a different route than her brother-in-law, heading beyond the gate-house and down the hill. He thought it unnecessary, all the secrecy and hiding, and though Allie had tried to explain her reasoning for insisting on it, she knew he didn't understand.

Allie wanted this. Needed this. It was the only thing she'd ever had that was hers and hers alone. No one had told her to train with Aidan. No one had even recommended it. She had come up with the idea on her own and persuaded him—with difficulty.

Indeed, when she'd first proposed the idea, Aidan had thought it a jest. She'd insisted it wasn't and asked him to choose a weapon for her to use.

His choice of the longsword had surprised her, but the need to use both hands actually made it a lighter choice than any other weapon, with the exception of a dagger. And she was even more surprised to discover she was good at it. Indeed, in the few weeks since they'd begun to train, she had improved enough to become an actual sparring partner.

She followed Aidan into the dense thicket. What little light remained was blocked by the trees' canopy.

Almost there.

They would have an hour, no more, before the evening meal was served. The meal promised to be a lively affair since Gillian and her new husband were preparing to host a council meeting, the first such affair they'd oversee as husband and wife. Clan chiefs, chieftains, and even the Lord Warden himself would soon descend on Highgate End.

"Something's wrong," Aidan correctly surmised when he saw her.

"I was thinking of the council."

Aidan cocked his head to the side. "What of it?"

She looked up into the warm, honest eyes of the man who'd quickly become her friend and confidante these past months. "We'll not be able to meet with so many people about."

Aidan rolled his eyes, something he often did with her, although Allie didn't take offense. He was playful by nature, one of his many endearing qualities.

"We shall see about that," he said. "Now come, lass, we've not much time."

Allie beamed, eagerly anticipating her favorite part of the day.

2

"You really should be more discreet in your attentions."

Reid tore his gaze away from the comely maid who was bent over the trestle table in front of them, beneath the raised dais. His sister-in-law was looking at him with more pity than concern.

"Why?" Reid asked. A glare from his brother told him that his tone was not appreciated. "That is to say"—Reid reached for the goblet in front of him—"why do you say so, Jules?"

Juliette had learned to tolerate him, and sometimes, though not at the moment, she even seemed to like him.

"The new maid did not arrive here alone," Juliette answered, gesturing to another woman at the back of the hall.

"You mean she has a sister," he said, staring at the face of the very woman Toren had pulled him away from a few evenings prior. For the first time that day, he smiled.

"Ugh. You are . . ."

Reid immediately flattened his lips. His amusement would only infuriate her further. "Despicable?" he finished for her.

"Predictable," she said.

He winked to soften the blow, and it worked. Juliette merely cast an ill-humored glance at Toren, shook her head, and returned to her meal.

"More importantly," his brother said, "is all readied for tomorrow?"

Reid drank deeply, watching both the maid Toren had deprived him of as well as her sister. Both tried, unsuccessfully, not to look his way. Where had they come from, anyway?

Not that it mattered.

"Reid?"

"Aye, Toren," he said, looking at his brother. "All is ready. Though I hardly think four men—"

"I'll not argue this again."

"Aye, Chief."

Toren glared at him, quite a statement given they were seated next to each other, while Juliette ignored them both. When she winced, Reid initially thought it was on account of him—until he noticed how quickly her hand moved to her stomach. He and Toren both shot up at once, and the next moment, they were kneeling beside her, one on either side.

"What is it?" Toren fairly shouted.

"Jules?" Reid watched helplessly as she took a deep breath. After what seemed like a lifetime, she smiled.

"Both of you," she admonished, "sit back down. 'Tis just the wee one letting me know she's there."

Reid and his brother exchanged a glance.

"Are you sure—"

"Aye, love," she said, splaying her fingers over Toren's hand on her stomach.

"Now sit," she said to Reid. "And eat. You've both a long journey ahead."

He glanced back down one last time, gauging her sincerity, and then returned to his seat.

"Do you suppose Linkirk will be in attendance?" Toren asked. Though the words were addressed to Reid, Toren continued to dart glances at his wife. They would all feel much better once the babe was safely delivered.

"You mean Clave?"

Toren took a bite of stew. "Linkirk, Clave. Though if you ask me, a man with an earldom in two countries is bound to be forced to choose his true loyalties eventually."

They all knew the current situation at the border between England and Scotland could not stand. For thirty years, a monthly Day of Truce, overseen by a warden chosen by each side, had ensured criminals on both sides of the border were brought to justice when needed. Over the last year, a series of escalating feuds, attacks, and other events had shaken that tried-and-true system. The Scottish warden had called a council meeting at Highgate End, a last effort to save the carefully cultivated peace, and Reid had agreed to attend in his brother's place. They hoped it would help shore up the peace, but he had doubts.

Every day the possibility of battle loomed larger. If it came to that, Clave would not be the only man forced to choose sides. Both of his brothers had married English women, and his sister an English lord . . . a folly he would be sure to avoid. Though they also had loyalty to their clans, their personal lives certainly complicated matters.

"The choice is not between Scotland and England," Juliette said. "'Tis between order and lawlessness."

"And when laws are broken?" He should not enjoy goading his sister-in-law. Despite his disdain for the English, even he had to admit they were not all bad.

"Justice should prevail."

"Hmm." Should. But it did not always. Which was precisely why the warden had called the council. The problem of a very crooked English warden was one that, unsolved, would doom the borderlands to the same unrest as before the Treaty of York.

"Enough," Toren said. "If we could resolve such issues here, there would be no need for the meeting."

Reid sat back and looked for the pretty blonde sisters, but they'd disappeared from sight.

"Just be safe," Juliette said. "And do not court trouble."

Ahh, he'd found her, the one he'd already tasted.

"Trouble?" he asked distractedly, anticipating the night ahead. "Never."

He ignored Juliette's laughter and sought out the woman's gaze. It wasn't difficult to attract her attention. The last great council had lasted weeks, and if Reid's memory served, there had been no maids at Highgate to amuse him.

Luckily, such was not the case this eve.

"You forgot to reorient the tip."

Allie sighed. Why did she forget every single time? "Perhaps you can show me a different method?"

Aidan crossed his arms. "Very well."

She brought her feet back into the starting position.

"Remember, you are aiming for my blade, not my body."

She tried to concentrate. Stood hips facing forward, sword at shoulder height. Brought it down decisively and—

Ouch!

Allie had remembered to reorient the tip of the blade, but she'd let her excitement distract her—so much so that Aidan was able to knock her blunted sword completely out of her hands.

When he bent down to retrieve it for her, she moved quickly, positioning herself away from his reach. Aidan always said her speed was a strength, so she tried to use it whenever possible.

"Nice recovery," he said, looking up at the darkening sky. "Though I do think we should return to the keep."

Allie watched as Aidan put his finger to his lips. He was looking off into the distance, but she didn't see anything there other than the tops of some very tall, old trees.

"What is it?" she whispered.

Aidan frowned at her, something that only made her more curious. She couldn't help it. Allie wanted to know what he saw. Or heard.

"Aidan?"

He gave her the same look he'd given her upon hearing her suggestion that they keep these training sessions secret. But she would not let his expression destroy her good mood.

"Likely an animal," he said finally. "Though if it had been anything else, you'd have given us away with all of that noise. 'Aidan,'" he mimicked in an exaggerated, breathy whisper.

"I did *not* sound like that."

He continued. "'Aidan. Aidan. Who's there? What's happening? Is it—'"

"You're quite amusing," she said, her tone suggesting just the opposite.

Due to the rolling hills, they had a clear view of Highgate Castle as they walked back beyond the dense tree line. In silent agreement, they both stopped and watched as another retinue of men on horseback arrived. The leaders of the various border clans had begun to descend on Highgate End two days ago for the planned summit. Allie could not help but feel a twinge of excitement for the days ahead. Of course, Gillian kept reminding her—every day, it seemed—that this was not a celebration. She knew that. Knew better than most the dangers that lurked on both sides of the border and the implications for her family back in England and Highgate End. Even still, the arrival of so many men, and even some of their ladies . . . how could she not be excited after twenty years of boredom at Lyndwood? Gillian would have told her that was an exaggeration—that she couldn't possibly remember being bored as a babe—but that was the way it felt.

"You're in good spirits." Aidan said, watching the riding party's procession. Then his eyes widened and his grin faded.

"What is it?"

He gestured up the hill. "I just recognized our new guests," he said. "Go ahead. I will be right behind you to greet the men of Clan Kerr."

With a nod, Allie began the long walk uphill. The guards, of course, knew she and Aidan trained nearly every evening. They had promised her brother-in-law not to mention the fact to anyone, though they likely thought her as silly as Aidan did. Allie didn't care.

Allie tried to imagine the look on her father's face if he were to find out what she was doing, and the image made her laugh aloud. She was still smiling when she entered the gatehouse and handed her sword to Aidan's friend Lawrence. He kept the longsword for her, and he kept her secret too. Lawrence nodded knowingly, and she thanked him before she continued on to the keep.

It was nearly time for the evening meal, and if she wished to escape the odd looks her unconventional outfit was sure to cause, Allie thought it best that she enter through Armorer's Tower rather than the main keep. She could reach her bedchamber from there.

A noise behind her made her turn back toward the gatehouse whence she'd come. The same men they'd seen earlier were exiting the stables as Aidan arrived to greet them. Allie could not see the men clearly, but she didn't think she recognized them. Of course, she did not know many people in Scotland, save those here at Highgate.

But that was about to change.

3

Reid sent the men ahead. He planned to return to the gatehouse to speak to the guards and ensure they were taking proper precautions. A gathering such as this occurred so rarely, and with Douglas in attendance along with so many of the clans' chiefs, there was danger of a targeted attack. If de Sowlis's men resented his line of questioning, so be it.

And that's when he saw her.

Though she looked his way, her gaze did not linger. From this distance, he could hardly see her face, but something about her caught his attention. Mayhap it was the boys' clothing she wore. He'd seen women dressed that way before, though it was not common. Such a thing would not normally intrigue him, but he wished to see what lay beneath the oversized tunic draped over her. As Reid approached, he could see her shape more clearly beneath the voluminous fabric. Her curves were all woman, and her thick, lustrous brown hair was braided down her back.

The woman had turned away from him, and without thinking it through, he found himself following. His speed was enough that he would overtake her before she reached the keep. He did not know what he planned to say, but inspiration would come to him.

It always did.

Her hips swayed as she walked, the brisk pace making him wonder at her destination. He'd assumed she headed toward the keep, but instead she turned toward an attached tower building, reaching for the iron handle of the small wooden door.

He grabbed it from behind and opened it for her.

"Oh!"

When she spun around, Reid sucked in his breath. His instincts, as always, had not let him down. He wanted her, this slip of a woman who walked as if she owned Highgate End. She looked at him with a mixture of astonishment and lust.

"I'm sorry," she said. "I did not see you behind me."

"Yet here I am."

She did not know how to respond, but *he* did.

"I would follow you anywhere, fair maid." He inclined his head to indicate she should continue inside.

"I . . ." She turned, peering into the entranceway. Her features were dainty for a lass who dressed as a man. "Are you looking for the hall?"

Reid didn't answer. He was not, and she knew it.

"I . . . I'm afraid I am returning to my chamber to prepare for the meal. You cannot—"

"Perfect," he said.

He expected a shy smile; she surprised him by frowning.

"Are you suggesting you would like to follow me there?"

Her speech marked her as a noblewoman. Though the revelation was disappointing—she was much less likely to entertain him —it did nothing to dampen his intrigue. Why was a noblewoman so oddly dressed?

"Only if you need an escort."

She opened her mouth, likely to deny him, but then closed it instead. Her expression indicated she would have slapped him on the face had her good manners not insisted otherwise. Damn. He had very much misjudged her. Not just a noblewoman then, but an innocent. Too bad, since she really would have been an enjoyable way to pass the time here at Highgate.

"Who are you?" he asked. The question had not mattered before, but it certainly did now.

"Are you always so . . . direct?"

"Always."

Her eyes narrowed. Their conversation had come to an end.

Pity.

"I am sister to Lady Gillian, wife of Graeme de Sowlis, chief of Clan Scott and—" she paused for effect, as if one were needed, "—your host."

Reid bowed, an exaggerated one sure to inflame her. Though why he goaded the lady, he didn't know.

"Reid Kerr," he said, leaving the introduction at that.

"I would say I'm pleased to meet you." Her eyes narrowed. "But I do not care to perjure myself."

Indeed. Reid might enjoy himself at Highgate after all.

"You will change your mind."

Eyes widening, she walked into the tower and left him holding the door. It was only as Reid watched her go that he realized she'd not told him her name.

No matter. He would find out soon enough.

<hr>

"If there is nothing else, my lady, your sister—"

"Go," Allie said. "And please tell Gillian I will be down shortly."

Morgan's very proper curtsy was followed by her quick exit. The lady's maid had attended to her and Gillian for years, and was as much a friend as she was a helper, yet she still insisted on politesse.

Dressed for the evening meal but not quite ready to attend it, Allie thought back to her meeting with Reid Kerr, the most handsome and most irritating man she'd ever met. When she'd first turned around, Allie had nearly been knocked over by the sheer force of him. It was a ridiculous notion, of course, but true nonetheless. His height and muscular frame, his self-assured smile and piercing eyes, his thick light brown hair—one could hardly take it all in at once.

Of course, he could tell how he affected her.

For a brief moment, as her heart hammered in her chest and Reid looked at her with open admiration, she felt on the cusp of doing something foolish. Her sister had engaged in a passionate embrace with a stranger, Graeme, only to find herself wedded and headed to Scotland in a mere two days. She'd struggled to understand how rational, proper Gillian had been induced to do such a thing.

She suddenly understood.

For if the circumstances had been different, the man less arrogant and more . . . more like Graeme, or even Aidan, she'd have done the same. That embarrassing fact was overshadowed by another. Reid Kerr was a complete and utter arse. She should be embarrassed by the vile language, even though she hadn't spoken the word aloud, but there was no other description that seemed to fit.

Standing, Allie took a deep breath and made her way from her chamber down a set of winding stone stairs. She could reach the main keep from the bottom floor of the tower or go back outside the way she had come. A moment later, finding herself in the same spot where she had first encountered the insufferable Scotsman, Allie chastised herself for a fool. Was she really looking for him? No, she was not. Certainly not. He'd be long gone.

And thank the saints for that.

Of course, he was very likely to appear in the great hall for the evening meal—the meal that was already well underway by the time Allie entered the main doors of the keep and ascended to the hall. The din of clanging mugs and the murmuring voices grew louder with each step. The center of all castle activity became more crowded every night, and according to Gillian, Highgate's hall would be filled to capacity by the time the meeting of the great council commenced in three days' time. They'd greeted guests at Lyndwood, of course, but never this many at once.

"Good to see I am not the only late arrival."

Allie jumped at the sound of Aidan's voice. By the time she turned around, he was watching her with the same look of concern he wore any time she or Gillian appeared unhappy.

"You really are the best brother a lady could acquire," she said sincerely.

"By marriage, of course," he said, holding out his arm.

She took it without thought and allowed him to escort her to the high table.

"Well?" he prodded. "You want to talk about what has you—"

"Shhh," she said, cutting him off—she would never, ever, admit what had shaken her—and turned to greet her sister.

"Gillian," she said. "Graeme."

They both murmured greetings. Gillian had been watching one of the musicians play the rebec, the stringed instrument whose soft, melodic sound had entranced both sisters from an early age.

"Gill," she said, lowering herself. "Do you remember the time I begged Father to allow me to learn to play?" Taking her usual seat between her sister and Aidan, she forced herself to concentrate on the company of her companions rather than looking out into the crowd.

"I do." Gillian's eyes sparkled with mischief. "And I also remember when you stole that poor man's instrument—"

"Borrowed," she cut in.

"My sister, the thief." Aidan winked at her as he nudged his goblet toward a servant making the rounds with a carafe of wine.

Allie did the same.

Before responding to the accusation, she picked up her wine and took a small sip. Her eyes darted toward the crowded room and then back. "Father, of course, refused to arrange for lessons. But I simply had to know if I could play as well as the musician did. It did not look overly difficult—"

"And was it?" Aidan asked.

She shook her head. "Not at all."

Gillian's laugh attracted more than a few stares. Allie hid her own smile behind the goblet as she took a more lingering sip.

"Shouldn't you ask those of us who had to listen?" Gillian said. "Mother caught her with it and gave the instrument back to its rightful owner. Thank the heavens. My poor ears—"

"Enough," Allie begged. "If Mother could have, just once, supported us over Father." She'd tried to say it lightly, as a jest, but the words had too much truth to them. "I will gladly let the musician provide the entertainment this eve."

When she looked back out into the hall this time, their eyes met.

Allie had spotted him moments before, three tables away from her, though she'd immediately looked away. The man was too large, too alive, to be ignored. Allie noticed two things at once. She was not the only woman in the hall looking at him. And his interest in her had not waned. If anything, his stares were even bolder. Though he was dressed simply, his deep green surcoat proclaimed him anything but common. A chief, perhaps?

"No."

She looked at Gillian. "Pardon?"

"Absolutely, not. Do not consider it, even for a moment."

Her sister had the attention of the entire head table. She gave her head a little shake as if to say, *We will discuss this later.* And proceeded to promptly change the topic.

No? Had Gillian seen her looking at Reid Kerr? It seemed likely. Her sister never missed even the smallest detail. If she *had* caught her looking—as she was doing surreptitiously now while pretending the just-served pigeon pie was the most fascinating thing she'd ever seen—then she clearly had a poor opinion of the man. An opinion that likely fit Allie's own observations.

Then why did it take every bit of self-restraint for her to eat her meal without looking his way?

"He is horrid." Gillian whispered the accusation between sips of wine. Clearly, her aversion to Reid was such that she couldn't wait to disparage him.

"I know."

And she did. Rather than allow him to distract her, she should concentrate on enjoying the meal and listening to the fine music Gillian had commissioned. She turned to do just that, only her eyes didn't heed her. They sought out Reid in the crowd. And he was still looking at her.

4

"Please, please, please tell me you were not looking at Reid Kerr *that* way."

Gillian had cornered her, waylaying her attempt to retire early. No longer hungry, she'd found it impossible to sit in that hall any longer. It was as if a swarm of butterflies had invaded the meal and were attempting fly up under her gown. Her hands shook and her head was filled with visions of the impossible Scotsman.

She had made it across the length of the hall, past their guests and nearly halfway through the corridor that led to the stairs, and freedom, before Gillian grabbed her arm from behind.

"*That* way?"

"I apologize," Gillian said, starting over. "I thought I saw him looking at you—"

"You did."

Gillian was unwittingly emulating the concerned look their mother gave them whenever they did not agree with their father. She would have pointed out the fact had her sister not appeared to be genuinely upset.

"We need to talk."

Her sister walked further away from the hall, toward the

attached chapel. Instead of entering it, she took the winding stairs to the wall-walk above. Apparently whatever she felt needed saying required absolute privacy.

Allie took a deep breath of air that was surprisingly still warm. The only sources of light were the torches in the towers they stood between and the stars and moon above.

"'Tis nearly full," she said of the waxing moon.

Gillian nodded. "It seems the council will be held during a new moon."

The moon had always fascinated Allie. Though she did not agree that the moon's shape at birth predicted one's character, she did wonder at its purpose and what it was made of.

"I met him once before, you know," Gillian said.

"Where?" She could not disguise the interest in her tone.

"At The Wild Boar, on our way back from our first visit to Lyndwood as a married couple."

Allie remembered the visit well. The awful man she'd agreed to marry, the one who'd gotten himself killed before they could wed, had *intended* to marry Gillian. He'd settled for Allie after Gillian was forced to marry Graeme. Rather than tell Gillian the truth—that she would go through with the wedding so their parents would not lose their home— she'd insisted she had a foolproof plan to avoid the match. She still felt poorly for lying to the person who cared for her most, who looked after her the way their mother should have, but if she'd allowed Gillian to spirit her away as her sister had intended, it would have caused problems for the new couple.

"I still feel poorly for lying to you," Allie began, but Gillian cut her off, shaking her head.

"You do not need to apologize. Again. I understand you were only trying to protect me. As I am doing for you now."

Allie shivered. She hated to think of what would have happened had the earl not—

"I met Reid," Gillian continued. "And took an immediate dislike to him. He is arrogant—"

"Aye, very."

"And disdainful."

"So I've noticed."

"In fact, I asked Graeme why he would have such a man as an ally."

Allie had wondered the very same thing. "What did he say?"

"That he had known Reid and his older brothers his entire life. It was their sister, Catrina, to whom he was promised."

Allie's eyes widened. "*That* Catrina?"

"Aye."

Graeme had once been betrothed to a childhood friend. Allie did not know much of the story beyond that they had, of course, never married.

"He claimed Reid is, beneath it all, a good man." Gillian did not look convinced, and neither was she.

"His brother is the chief?"

"Aye. The middle brother, Alex, was once the chief's second, but he and his wife took up residence at Dunmure Tower, where the boys were raised."

"How do you know so much about him?" Allie stepped closer to the wall and laid a hand on the cool, gray stone.

"From Sara. She told me about the family, and Catrina, when Graeme and I . . ." Her sister paused.

Allie did not mean to laugh. But she so loved to tease her sister about the circumstances surrounding her first encounter with Graeme. "Encountered each other in the garden?"

Gillian smiled, taking the jest as easily as she did each time. "Aye."

"Well," Allie said. "You've no cause for concern. He's merely curious. I met him earlier, in the courtyard, and was taken aback by his . . ." There were so many things she could say. Allie settled for, "Arrogance."

"Very well." Gillian looked back toward the hall. "I really should go—"

"Attend to your guests. I believe I shall retire early."

Gillian looked like she wished to say more, but having made her argument against Reid, one Allie took seriously, she simply smiled and bid her a good night.

Allie turned back toward the moon, staring at it once again. It fascinated her that her parents saw the very same moon when they looked up into the sky. Was her father easier to tolerate now that he no longer worried about their home being taken? More importantly, how much longer could she pacify him and his attempts to see her "safely wed"?

"Good evening, Lady Allie."

Thank goodness the wall in front of her was higher than her waist. Otherwise, she may have toppled over it, so startled was she at the deep, unwanted voice.

"I never told you my name." She turned slowly, addressing the man who'd so offended her sister at The Wild Boar.

"I know many things about you now that I did not know when we first met."

The dark blue of her surcoat blended with the night sky, making the long, pale slope of her neck and elegant hands even more pronounced. He could hardly see much of her upon his initial approach. Now that she'd turned fully toward him, Reid could see the lady quite well.

He waited, and she did not disappoint him.

"Such as?"

It was simply too easy.

"You live here with your sister and her husband, though some believe the stay is temporary. Apparently Lord Lyndwood believes his youngest daughter is well past marriageable age. You've seen a few more than twenty summers?"

She didn't answer.

"I believe you have."

"I believe it is time for you to leave."

Reid frowned. "Have I offended you in some way, my lady?"

Though he clearly had, she did not move to abandon him.

Yet.

"Why are you up here?"

He took a step toward her, the smell of rose petals wafting toward him as he moved. "The same reason you are, I suspect."

Well aware that he was walking a fine line, Reid stopped his approach and abruptly turned his back to the wall and leaned against it.

"I was speaking privately with my sister."

"About me?"

The look on her face said it all. She wanted to rail against him, push him out of the way and leave. Surprisingly, she did not. Yet her expression hardly changed.

"Do you always believe you are the subject of conversation?" Her hands gestured in the air as she spoke. She may have been raised a proper English noblewoman, but she had a bit of spirit in her.

"No," he said. "Though I could not help but notice your attention during the meal—or that your sister gave me some very unwelcoming glances."

She lifted her chin. "You met her once before."

"Aye," he said. "Unaccountably, I don't believe she likes me much."

She smiled, and even though her lips had a mocking tilt, his hardened heart began to beat wildly.

"Finally, an astute observation."

Reid crossed his arms. "I fear I am at a loss to explain her lack of warmth toward me."

Again, that smile.

"Much as I am at a loss to explain how her husband believes you redeemable."

He'd not have used that word, but Reid was surprised nonetheless. He would have imagined Graeme de Sowlis saw him much the same as most did . . . as Toren and Alex's younger brother, and nothing more.

He pushed away from the wall so abruptly, Allie looked as if she would back away. But she did not. Reid took a step, and then another, toward her. The air between them sizzled, and Reid knew he was entering dangerous territory.

Caution, unfortunately, had never been one of his favored traits.

"I fear we should start over." Reid was sure she would pull her hand away when he reached out to grab it, but again she surprised him. Her fingers, cool from the air yet smooth and soft, lay still in his own. He brought them to his lips and instantly cursed himself. His cock was rock-hard by the time he pressed his lips to her hand. The reaction he'd hoped to elicit was from her, not him.

With effort, he dropped her hand.

"I am Reid Kerr, brother to the chief of Clan Kerr, and honored to make your acquaintance."

"You are?" She clearly did not trust him to behave.

Smart woman.

When she opened her full lips to speak again, Reid hoped she would challenge him. Curse him. Tell him to leave and never speak to her again. Anything but that, and he would be undone. He'd not expected himself to react this strongly to her.

And he didn't like it. He would much rather be in control.

"My name is Lady Allie, daughter of John Bowman, Lord Lyndwood, and sister to the lady of Highgate End."

He smiled. That was better.

"Regretfully, however, I am not honored to make *your* acquaintance."

With that, she left.

Leaving Reid to laugh with none but the guards in the distance to hear the sound.

5

*R*eid allowed the raised voices around him to meld into one tedious drone. Although the official council would not be held for two more days, after the Lord Warden arrived, those already in attendance sat in their hosts' solar doing what clan chiefs do best.

Arguing.

Though each of them was in attendance for the same purpose, to secure continued peace along the border, opinions on how to achieve such a goal varied widely. They only agreed on one point: the current climate could not continue. The recent increase in the number and severity of attacks along the border worried leaders on both sides of the divide. At least, those who were not using the instability to bribe their way to greater financial gain.

Until Douglas arrived, none of their talk mattered.

"Does Clan Kerr agree?"

Ferguson MacDuff asked, pulling Reid's attention back to the debate.

"Do you care if we do or do not?" he asked.

While his brothers would chastise him for poking an already angry chieftain, Reid simply could not resist. MacDuff and de

Sowlis were allies, but he would never forget the former's reluctant response to Toren's call for help after Catrina was taken by the English.

MacDuff's face turned an even brighter shade, much like his red hair. "You insult me to ask such a question."

The seven other men in the room watched their exchange closely.

"If an insult was given, none was intended," he said, keeping his voice as cool as MacDuff's was hot.

MacDuff's eyes narrowed. "You wonder why the elders hesitate to name you as your brother's second."

Reid could see Graeme was about to intervene, but he couldn't let him do it. He needed to be sure MacDuff, and the others in attendance, were all clear on that particular topic.

"I could never replace Alex," he said of his brother. No truer words had ever been spoken, at least not by him. And he knew better than anyone that the truth was oft more uncomfortable than any lie.

It worked.

MacDuff snapped his mouth closed. His argument had been stolen from him, and he hesitated to so openly agree with the man he was chastising.

"To answer your question," he continued, "Clan Kerr is in full agreement. The appointment of Lord Caxton as the English warden will certainly not ease tensions."

"Caxton," another clan chief spat. "There is not a man alive who hates us more. And so unlike Hallington."

Juliette's father may have sheltered his daughter, a common enough occurrence along the border, but his failing health was felt by all when he was forced to remove himself as warden. Fair and well-respected, with the exception of a misunderstanding that had put his brother Toren in an awkward position when he first met his future wife, Hallington's replacement was a very different sort of man.

"Aye," Graeme said. "I fear the repercussions are already being felt. But will Douglas be willing to act?"

An uncomfortable silence met the question. None knew how their Lord Warden, a fair and honorable man, would react to the Englishman's appointment. The Treaty of York, formed more than thirty years earlier, dictated their current state of affairs. It had established a border between Scotland and their southern neighbors and instituted the monthly Day of Truce. It was all that stood between them and abject, uncontrolled violence.

Someone accused the English of inventing titles to preserve their self-importance—as if they did not do the same—and Reid stopped listening again. Their ranting would go on for hours. Toren often complained about such gatherings, and Reid could see why. He allowed his thoughts to drift to a certain brown-haired Englishwoman who had captured not only his attention but his dreams.

Reid had awoken that morn primed and ready, and it had only taken a moment for him to remember why. Lady Allie. Last eve she was a very different woman than the one he'd first met outside the tower. Why had she dressed in boys' clothing? And where had she been rushing to, or from, when she'd first gripped his attention and refused to let go?

The questions, and the lady, were so engrossing that it took him a moment to realize the bickering had stopped and the others had begun to stand. He started to do the same, surprised but delighted they were finished already, when de Sowlis nodded to him, indicating he wished for a private word outside the chamber. Unfortunately, it appeared the men were merely taking a break.

He followed Graeme out of the chamber, expecting to be chastised about his treatment of MacDuff. Instead, the man seemed almost . . . nervous.

"This is awkward for me, Reid," he began.

Now he was even more curious.

"I do not typically meddle in such affairs."

Reid waited and watched as Graeme's eyes darted sideways. It struck him that this conversation would have nothing to do with MacDuff. Or their discussions.

This was about Allie.

His brother Alex had often said if he believed in witchcraft, he would think his own brother practiced such sorcery. The truth was less exciting. He merely observed more than most.

"Gillian worries, some may say overly much, for her sister."

Reid tried hard not to smirk. Offending Graeme would infuriate Toren, so he simply pretended not to understand. "I should think so. She is, as I understand it, her older sister."

Graeme smiled. "You know how protective an older sibling can be."

"Protective? Nay. Toren only has half of Clan Kerr at my back when I travel more than a day's ride away from Brockburg," he joked.

"Then you understand . . ."

He liked Graeme, but he was not going to make this so easy on him. "Understand what, Graeme?"

"Allie seems to have . . . taken an interest in you."

Reid's pulsed raced at the possibility. He believed so as well, but she'd so easily dismissed him . . . "And your wife does not wish to encourage such an . . . interest?"

Reid did not need an answer. He already had one. But he wouldn't lie to his host by promising to do something he was incapable of doing.

"Are you asking me to stay away from her?" he added.

He was, of course. But Graeme was nothing if not well-mannered. He would not offend him by saying as much outright. "She will not take kindly to you, Reid."

"I've no doubt you are right."

"She is unmarried. And very much an innocent."

Reid held Graeme's gaze. "I am aware."

"And you—"

"Again, I am aware."

"So quick to assume. Reid, I've known you for many years. You are a fierce warrior and as loyal as any man."

That did manage to surprise him.

"I ask only you tread carefully here."

"Understood," he said, aware of the difficult position Graeme was in because of him.

"Good," Graeme said. "We should return then." As his host edged his way back to the solar, Reid remained in the corridor, considering the conversation. Graeme had not warned him away, but neither had he encouraged his advances. He'd done his duty to his wife, and if Reid were smart, he would heed the warning, however implicit.

He could not bed a woman such as Lady Allie unless he wanted to bring a bride back to Brockburg, which he certainly did not. But something about her compelled him, and if he was unwilling to lie to Graeme, he certainly would not do so to himself.

He'd no less avoid Lady Allie than the clan chiefs in that room would avoid a confrontation with the new warden. In fact, now seemed like the perfect time to find his fair English maid to learn exactly how kindly she would take to him today.

"I SHOULD BE MEETING with the others." Aidan put down his own training sword and handed Allie a waterskin. She drank deeply, for the day was warmer than most, and tossed it on the ground.

"How could we not take advantage of the reprieve?" she asked, lifting the sword in front of her with both hands. A lavish dinner was being served after the meeting, and the men had been given leave to forgo their training for the remainder of the afternoon. Which had given her the opportunity to meet Aidan for a longer training session.

"It is likely over by now," she said, placing her left foot forward and getting into position. "Though are you sure you do not wish to prepare for the meal?" Allie adjusted her grip and lifted the sword in front of her.

"My stomach can wait. Your defeat cannot."

With that, Aidan made the first move, which Allie countered by blocking him with her sword.

"Good," he said, pulling back. "Your turn."

By the time Aidan stopped again for another break, Allie was breathing heavily, pleased with her progress.

"You're a fine instructor, Master Aidan," she said, picking the waterskin back up from where she'd discarded it earlier.

"Thank you," he said, offering her a mock bow.

Allie laughed easily, as she'd always done with Aidan. Not long after they'd met, he'd taken to calling her "little sister," and it fit. They had gotten along from the start, and Allie couldn't be more grateful for his help. And for his discretion.

"Thank *you*."

Aidan moved his sword from one hand to the other. "For?"

"For this." She gestured to her sword. "For giving me something of my own."

Aidan frowned. "I can't imagine what it must have been like—"

"Let us not talk about Covington."

Belatedly, Allie realized he wasn't speaking of the Earl of Covington but of her father. She'd told Aidan enough that he pitied her, though she did not want anyone's pity. In his own way, her father loved her and her sister. And at least her parents were alive. The relationship could improve. She felt poorly complaining about her parents when Aidan's were both gone.

"Shall we talk about—"

Aidan rushed at her so quickly, Allie did not have time to think. When it registered that this was not part of their training session, she peered around him to see what he protected her from.

A figure came into view. It was a man. Nay, not just a man.

Him.

The one who refused to leave her thoughts, even as she slept, despite her sister's warnings and her own assessment of him. Allie had awoken that morning from a dream in which his face was in front of hers, his taunting smirk in place, and his lips . . .

"Reid." Aidan put down his sword and moved away from her. "What are you doing here?"

Though Aidan spoke to him, Reid Kerr was looking directly at her.

He was here because of her. She knew it as well as she knew her own name.

"It seems I'm not the only one who has already had enough of the daily bickering," Reid replied.

"Allow me to introduce you to—"

"We've met," she interrupted.

Reid looked down at her sword. Now she would actually have to speak civilly to him, convince him to keep her training sessions between them.

"A longsword." He moved toward her, and Allie fought the instinct to back away. He was dangerous, of that there was no doubt. "May I?"

She looked at Aidan, who nodded. When he and his men arrived, Aidan had recognized him. But how well did the two men know each other? Did Aidan share Gillian's opinion of the man?

Allie handed the blunted weapon to him.

"What does a lady need with such a weapon?"

Allie made a sound that brought a smile to Aidan's face. She supposed it was not very ladylike, but nothing about her was lady-like just now, from her leggings and oversized linen shirt to the old leather belts keeping it from hanging too low.

"You would not understand."

Reid appeared to be impressed by the weapon. "You may be surprised."

Since he was getting no answers from her, Reid looked at

Aidan, who was much more forthcoming. No doubt he'd been dying to tell someone.

"I am training her," he said. "Though the lady would prefer to keep the fact quiet."

"Hmm," he responded noncommittally.

Aidan turned toward her. "Reid has somewhat of a reputation—"

"I'm sure he does," she blurted.

The man in question laughed. Allie had not heard him laugh before, and she wasn't sure she liked it. His self-satisfied smirk was much more fitting. When he laughed, Reid Kerr looked almost . . . human.

Aidan looked back and forth between them and continued. "A reputation as a swordsman. And as a man to avoid in battle, though luckily, we have fought only for the same side. Though I'm not sure of his skill with this particular weapon."

Reid held her sword up in front of him.

"May I?" he asked her.

It took Allie a moment to realize what he meant to do. But when Aidan lifted his own sword, she backed away.

"Of course," she said, crossing her arms in satisfaction. He would have proceeded without her permission, no doubt, but she was anxious to see Aidan best their unwelcome guest. Her brother-in-law was known for his skill with the dagger, but he was equally as skilled with the longsword.

The loud clash of metal hitting metal echoed all around them. If they were nearer the castle, people would gather to watch the two men spar with each other. A match between two such braw men would have been entertaining were it not so terrifying.

Even though both weapons were blunted, Allie had seen more than one knight being carried off the training yard with injuries ranging from minor scratches to life-threatening gashes.

In fact, she was about to yell for the men to stop when Reid's sword clashed so forcefully with Aidan's that her brother-in-law's weapon went flying into the air. He retrieved it quickly enough, but the match was over.

Aidan whistled. "It appears the rumors are true."

Some men would be bitter at having been bested, but Aidan appeared to take it in stride. Would Reid? Somehow, she did not think so.

When he looked at her, Allie's breath caught. He was certainly bolder than any man she'd ever met. More arrogant and definitely more—

"Let me train her."

She froze.

Aidan looked back and forth between them. "Reid, I don't believe—"

"There is no one better."

He was not jesting!

"You are needed up there"—Reid nodded toward the castle —"more than I. Until I leave, let me train—"

"Pardon," she said, interrupting his very pretty speech. "The woman in question is standing here, listening to your conversation."

She may have been quite sheltered for most of her life, but she was not completely addled. And she certainly would not let Reid make decisions for her as if she were not present.

"He is quite good—" Aidan started. One glance at her, and he quickly backtracked. "But Allie is right. It is up to her, not me."

She did not need to consider it for long. "Then the choice is an easy one—"

"Although if Reid trained you, I could more easily assist Graeme."

Allie looked at Aidan as if he'd gone mad. What was he doing? Why would he agree with such a brute?

"Then it is settled."

"'Tis not settled." Allie put her hands on her hips and glared at both men. Her brother-in-law had gone daft and Reid . . . he was simply the most infuriating man she'd ever met in her life.

"Give me one reason I should agree to such a thing," she taunted him.

Reid took a step toward her, and then another. Her heart thudded in her chest as he moved ever closer, and she had to remind herself to breathe.

He handed the sword back to her and said, loud enough that only she could hear, "Because you want me to."

6

If there was a bigger fool in Scotland, Reid didn't know him. There was no good reason for what he'd just done. He was impulsive, thoughtless. Wasn't that exactly why the elders had expressed concern about appointing him as Toren's second? If he were another, better, man . . .

It seemed she was as much a fool as he because, unbelievably, she was going to agree.

Reid had gone off looking for Allie after the meeting, and when he saw her and Aidan rushing through the courtyard, he'd been curious enough to follow. The sight of them walking into the nearby woods had turned Reid's curiosity into something more. Something, if he were being honest, that had led him to make an offer that was anything but wise and would surely lead to trouble.

Jealousy was not an emotion to which he was accustomed.

Allie raised her chin, the fire in her eyes another reason Reid wanted to take over her training. Why was she doing this? What compelled a noblewoman to wish to fight?

"Very well." And then she whispered for his ears only. "But only because it will be easier for him. Not because I believe it to be a good idea."

She referred to her brother-in-law, and once again Reid wondered about the nature of their relationship. What exactly was Aidan de Sowlis to her? A brother-in-law only? Something more? Did it matter?

He should not ask. "Are you sure?" The words left his lips despite himself.

"Aye," she answered, her voice strong.

He reached out his hand toward Aidan. "May I?"

The younger de Sowlis brother handed Reid his training sword, then stepped back and crossed his arms, leaning against a nearby tree. Why was he smiling? Apparently the two brothers had not spoken yet, and Reid wondered if, when they did, these training sessions would come to quick halt.

When Reid turned to face his new student, she was already in position. He took the opportunity to assess how much she'd learned so far.

"Show me how you move forward, or backward, with a series of cuts."

She did as instructed, and Reid watched to see if the side of each cut corresponded with her forward foot. It did, and he couldn't help but be impressed. He looked over at Aidan, who was clearly pleased by her skill.

"Well done," he said. After a series of moves, Aidan finally stopped them, and the lady's face fell.

"Already?" she asked, clearly disappointed.

"I should find Graeme—"

"Go," Reid said. "We will be along."

With a distinctly "Graeme" expression, Aidan tried to assess the lady's safety. He'd known the man his whole life . . . Hellfire, they'd almost become family.

"She will be safe with me."

Aidan frowned. "I know she will—"

"Then there is nothing to fear. Ask your brother."

At Aidan's confused expression, he said, "We had a discussion earlier today."

He looked at Lady Allie then, knowing he'd be forced to explain. So be it. But he saw her give a slight nod to her brother-in-law.

Though Aidan was clearly not prepared to listen to him, he did defer to his sister-in-law. "I am trusting you, Reid," he said, his meaning clear.

Then he left, not waiting for a response.

"What did Graeme say to you?" She'd turned the longsword upside down, its tip in the ground and her grip comfortable on its handle. And it was in that moment that Reid knew, unequivocally, he'd made a mistake. It would not be his last, but it was one he would have to live with until this council was over.

"Why did you agree to let me train you?" he shot back.

"What did he say to you?" she repeated.

Reid smiled, enjoying himself.

"Why do you laugh at me?"

"Laugh? I merely smiled. If that is a grave offense against your person, I do apologize."

She ignored that. "What do you find so amusing? And what did Graeme say to you?"

"Give me a boon, and I will answer both questions."

Had she known how to best him with the weapon in her hands, she'd have lifted it against him. He very much looked forward to their training sessions.

"Has anyone ever told you that you are a complete arse?"

He raised his brows. "Many times."

"You enjoy being told so. Why? Why would anyone revel in a reputation such as yours?"

"That, my lady, is a question not so easily answered. But if you permit me to use your given name, the answers to your first two questions are yours."

"You are—"

"I know it well," he finished for her. "May I call you Allie?"

It was forward of him, though no more so than taking over her training or being here, and she knew it well.

"Very well, *Reid*." Though she tried to make his name sound like poison on her lips, it was the sweetest sound he'd heard all day.

Reid took a step toward her, willing her not to move. When she did not, he halted his advance. "Graeme advised me to avoid you, though I believe he was simply following your sister's orders. Or perhaps not, since he knows me well. As to your second question, I smiled because you reminded me of my sister. She wears something similar"—he indicated her leggings—"courtesy of my sister-in-law, Lady Sara, who defies convention nearly as often as Catrina. When you gaze at me like that—as if you'd like to boil my bollocks for supper—you remind me of her."

He thought she might be shocked by his language, but she was not. Instead, she threw back her head and laughed so hard Reid could not help but smile alongside her.

"You forget my sister is Sara's oldest and dearest friend. I've heard of Catrina from her. Thank you for the compliment. As for Gillian . . ." Allie took a deep breath. "She can be . . . protective."

Reid resisted the urge to toss back a glib comment and said instead, "I know the sentiment well."

She thought about that for a moment. "Your brothers?"

A topic he did not wish to explore at that moment. "As for your first lesson . . ." He took another step forward, and this time she did move back, if only slightly. "You will need to do better than that."

"What lesson? You—"

"When I taunted you, you allowed me to discern your emotions."

"But I didn't realize—"

"Your opponent must never know you are scared, even if you are terrified. You must never back away unless there is a purpose for the movement." He indicated her feet. "As you just did from me."

Though she listed toward him, Allie wasn't ready for the lesson.

"I am not afraid of you," she said as confidently as she was able.

He took another step toward her, and this time it had nothing to do with her training.

"You should be."

SHE'D FAILED.

He could see through her bravado. Allie had lost control the moment she'd agreed to train with him, and she had no idea how to get it back. She certainly couldn't ask her sister. She would just have to pretend he didn't affect her. That the idea of him taking one step closer, so close he could reach out and touch her . . .

What have I done?

Gillian would kill her.

Allie wished she could reiterate her claim that she was not afraid of Reid Kerr, but she couldn't do so with any conviction. It was not true. She'd never been so afraid of a man, or more precisely, of her lack of control with one, in her life.

She hated him. Despised his attitude. Wanted to slap him every time the corner of his lip curled up in a smirk. And yet . . .

"Every emotion is there for me to see," he said finally. "Fear is weakness. A skilled swordsman—"

"Woman."

"A skilled swordsman, or woman, would rather fight without a weapon than show such weakness. Now try again."

She glared at him, which was not difficult, and refused to move her feet. He took another step toward her. If she lifted her arm, they would be touching.

"Better." He moved closer still. So close she could smell sandalwood, the musky scent entirely too appealing. His gaze did not waver.

She couldn't do it. He was too . . . intense.

Aye, Allie. You can. He's right. Fear is weakness.

Another step. He was so close now she had to look up to see his face. Though he did not have a beard, his stubble would feel rough beneath her fingers. His lips, the only soft feature on his face, parted ever so slightly. She swallowed, nearly looking away until she remembered something. A conversation with her sister.

If she'd managed to lie convincingly to Gillian, the person she knew better than anyone, then she had the strength to stand her ground with him. To pretend he did not move her.

When he realized she wasn't going to back away, he smiled. A real smile, for the first time.

That's when she lost her composure.

"'Tis not fair," she whispered, looking away. "I was doing well—"

"Exceedingly well."

The pricking of the shirt against her breasts was not something she had noticed before, but now it was all she could think of. Well, not the only thing . . .

He stepped back.

Able to breathe once again, Allie chastised herself for the unreasonable disappointment that bubbled up inside of her. He'd done as he should, backing away from her—

"Why did you look away?"

She'd thought back to that moment. "You smiled," she said simply.

"I've smiled at you before." He took another step back.

"But it was not like the others." She should have just said, *That one was real*. But even though he'd been completely horrible to her, with the glaring exception of his offer to train her, she could not bring herself to insult him just now.

"You looked away because you were surprised," he said as he

took another step back. Lifting the sword at his side, Reid moved into position. "Surprise can knock a man off his horse in a joust. It kills men in battle. Surprise is always your enemy. Which is precisely why we train so much."

"Woman," she said, placing her left foot forward, her legs still wobbly from the interaction.

"You thought of something," he said. "Something that strengthened your resolve."

He swung the sword down, and she blocked it with her own.

"My sister," she said as they moved back into position. Just like Aidan, he would only allow for one movement at a time so each could be honed to perfection. "I remembered the only time I'd ever been forced to lie to my sister."

Another thrust, another block.

"Why were you forced to lie to her?" he asked between moves.

"'Tis complicated." This time, she was able to block him even sooner than before.

"As it tends to be between siblings."

Again and again they practiced the same move.

"How much do you know about my sister and Lord Covington?" Allie asked, keenly aware that it might be another test.

"I know she was betrothed to him, and that she and Graeme married after being caught in a compromising position."

Allie laughed despite knowing she was at a disadvantage for doing so. "Most people put it more delicately than that."

He stopped suddenly, and she did the same. "I am not most people."

Of that, she was aware.

Allie was breathing heavily and, grateful for the break, forged ahead with her story. "When Gill left for Scotland, my father promised I would marry Covington in her stead."

She'd managed to surprise him.

"I'd not heard that."

She shrugged, pretending it had not mattered that her father had attempted to pledge both his daughters to an old man whose alliances along the border were questionable, his character even more so.

"Aye," she continued. "As you are likely aware, he was killed. And so the wedding never took place."

"And the conversation you referenced?"

"My sister came to Lyndwood desperate to save me from the match. I was forced to lie to her. I told her I had a plan to get out of the marriage."

It took him a moment to understand.

"But you had no such plan?"

"Nay. Only a desire for the happiness of the one person who loved me above all. Which she'd not have had if she had gone back to Scotland knowing I was to be wed to Covington."

"You'd have sacrificed yourself for her."

Her answer was swift. "Always."

Reid looked at her with a combination of curiosity and reverence, a look that made her want to take back her words.

"The bond between siblings . . . it is a gift, is it not?"

It wasn't his words that surprised her, but Reid's soft tone. It suited him.

"Very much," she said, thinking of the many times her sister had loved and protected her. "You would have done the same," she surmised, knowing it was true. This man would lay down his life for his sister and brothers.

"I would," was all he said, but his lack of any further explanation did not matter. What did matter was that she suddenly saw him. When Allie told him of her desire to see Gillian happy, she saw Reid Kerr for the first time. It was a fleeting glimpse. A brief flash of vulnerability—there and then gone. His mask was already firmly in place.

But that vulnerability had been there.

She'd seen it, and now she knew there was more to him than he allowed others to see.

7

*R*eid had taken advantage of the bath that had been offered to each visitor. The water had grown cold quickly, and though he was accustomed to chilly water from bathing at home in the frigid stream that ran from north to south at Brockburg, he was anxious to make his way to the hall.

To see her again.

Reid looked around the small but well-appointed guest chamber in Bronwen Tower. Years ago, when he was but a young boy, he'd stayed in this same tower as a guest, but he hadn't given Highgate End much thought after that. Not during the fissure between his clan and Clan Scott, and not after the alliance had been renewed. He certainly hadn't thought this would be where he'd meet the lass who would challenge his conviction to remain single.

Reid liked both of his sisters-in-law well enough, but he enjoyed his role as the younger, unwed brother. Not that he was considering marriage to Lady Allie. Certainly, he was not. Still, he could not deny that the woman captivated him, in a way that went far beyond a physical attraction.

Easily finding his way through the castle's semidarkened

corridors and into the courtyard, Reid walked under the pentice toward the great hall. He preferred using the covered walkway to winding his way through the pantry and kitchen.

A mist filled the air, threatening rain.

"Reid."

Aidan de Sowlis.

Reid had expected a talk with him this evening. In fact, he was anxious to speak to the man. He turned.

The younger de Sowlis brother was not much like him. Both of them had been left in the care of their older brothers at a young age. But the similarities stopped there. Most knew Aidan as a kind yet fierce warrior. None would describe Reid that same way, at least not using the word "kind."

"De Sowlis."

"We need to talk."

The mist began to morph into a light rain. And though they were covered, a spray of water made its way to them.

"In the hall?"

"Nay, here." His jaw locked and brows drawn, Aidan's expression implied he may have spoken to his brother. Would he change his mind about Allie's training?

"Aye, here then," he said. Those remaining in the courtyard scattered, finding shelter against the strengthening downpour. He waited for Aidan to guide their conversation.

"Tis good to see you again."

Reid had always liked both de Sowlis brothers and replied honestly. "And you, de Sowlis."

"Is it true you saved Toren—"

"Not I," he said, recalling the incident as he'd done more than once since arriving. "My clansmen."

Aidan's eyes narrowed as if he did not believe him. But it was true, in Clan Kerr, no one was blamed or praised for their individual feats.

"Very well." Aidan paused. "What are your intentions regarding Lady Allie?"

As was his custom, Reid's response was to offer an honest answer. "I don't know."

Aidan frowned, clearly not liking that answer. "Not good enough."

"If you want me to stay away from her, agreeing to let me train her does not seem—"

"Stay away from her?" Aidan appeared genuinely confused.

"Your brother spoke to me earlier. On his wife's behalf." He attempted to temper the words with a smile. "I apparently did not make a good first impression on the lady of Highgate."

Aidan didn't share in his amusement. "Unusual for you, is it not? With a woman at least."

"Most unusual," he agreed. "Although it seems to be a family trait."

"If Allie truly did not care for you, I'd never have agreed. Or left you there with her." He shrugged. "Even with a man whom I've personally witnessed risking his life to save another."

They'd fought together more than once, though Reid did not know the particular incident to which Aidan referred. "You asked for me to share my intent, but what is your own? Why leave the lady alone, and vulnerable, with me?"

Aidan didn't answer for a time.

Reid waited.

"Allie is not as vulnerable as you think," he said finally. "And I did it for the simple reason that she wanted me to. Even if she said otherwise."

Aidan spoke in riddles.

"And you are better with the longsword than I," he added.

"We can agree on that, at least."

"I ask again, what are your—"

"And I answered you already, Aidan. I'd not dishonor her, if that's what you're asking."

Aidan's eyes narrowed. "I would not expect it. But that isn't what worries me."

"Then what—"

"She has been sheltered most of her life and deserves a bit of adventure. But she does not deserve to have her heart broken by a man—"

"Aidan, you get ahead of yourself. I've agreed to train her, nothing more." Even as he said the words, Reid recognized the lie.

"And I agreed to it because of the way she looks at you. I think of her as my true sister. All I ask is that you remember that fact."

Reid really should forget he'd ever met Allie. Give her training back to Aidan, spend his afternoons listening to the bickering of the border chiefs, and go back to Brockburg when the council was over.

Unfortunately, he could not do that.

"You have my word," he said. "But your other sister-in-law—"

For the first time since their conversation began, Aidan smiled. "Allie can handle her sister," he said. "I worry more about your intentions."

Rightly so.

"I said I will not dishonor her, and I will not."

He had been warned. Twice. Only a fool would continue down a path that would lead to his own destruction.

And yet, he hastened to the great hall just the same.

He'd been watching her all evening. Yet if she paid him any more attention than the occasional surreptitious glance, Gillian would attempt to lock her in her bedchamber until the council was over. Proud of her effort to avoid looking his way, Allie was about to take a bite of the stewed partridge when Aidan whispered, "He is sitting just to the left of the sideboard."

Of course she looked. As if she had not already known where Reid was sitting.

"You are the worst sort of scoundrel."

Aidan leaned back, apparently pleased with himself.

"He is not very subtle," Aidan answered.

"Shhh." She glanced at her sister, who was speaking intently with her husband.

"She didn't hear me." Aidan reached for the salt cellar, an elaborate silver piece that had been a fixture of the head table for generations, according to Gillian. "So tell me, how did it go after I left?"

Darting another careful glance at Gillian, Allie told Aidan about the remainder of her afternoon. Increasingly uneasy about keeping her training sessions from her sister, Allie had actually planned to tell her, but now that Reid was her teacher . . .

"I believe we should continue to keep the sessions private for now." Allie nodded to her left.

"I should think so," Aidan said, wiping his fingers on the small linen cloth at his side. He lowered his voice once again. "She is not alone in her assessment of him, you know."

Allie watched Aidan's expression carefully. "You dislike him?"

Aidan sighed and looked straight at the man in question, who was now in deep conversation with the others at his table. "I did not say that."

Allie waited for him to continue.

"I believe Re—"

"He," she interrupted, not wanting Aidan to say his name aloud even though they were speaking in low voices.

"He," Aidan corrected. "I believe he is a good man, a respected warrior, who has yet to find his place."

"I don't understand."

Aidan smiled at the maid who brought a new jug of wine to their table. "When his older brother married and moved to

Dunmure Tower, there was immediately talk of *him* being named second."

Allie smiled, grateful for Aidan's discretion.

"Some say he doesn't want it. Others believe the clan elders won't allow it. Though no one knows the truth." Aidan shrugged. "As I said, he does have somewhat of a—"

He cut himself off and gave her a look.

Allie hated that look.

"You were about to say something to insult my young, delicate English ears," she said. She may have more freedom at Highgate than she did in Lyndwood, but she was still treated as a child sometimes.

"A reputation with women."

"Oh my," she mocked, holding her hands to her ears. "Not that. However will I recover? My tender sensibilities have been damaged beyond repair."

Aidan laughed.

"You must share the jest," Gillian said, turning toward them.

"Aidan has been taking lessons from you, dear sister, on how not to insult my innocence."

Gillian and Graeme exchanged a very different kind of look— one full of affection and something more—and Allie groaned aloud.

She appealed to Aidan. "You may stay to witness this display," she teased, "but I must excuse myself for a moment. 'Twill be a long night," she said, indicating the musicians in the corner of the hall.

"My lady," Aidan said, standing. "Until your return."

Allie made her way through the hall, smiling and nodding to the few familiar faces, careful not to glance *his* way. She picked up the hem of her favorite royal blue gown, the heavy velvet suited more for winter, and made her way toward the nearest garderobe.

She must not have been gone for very long. On her way back, Allie swore the same song was being played, the pipe and tabor a reminder of her youth in Lyndwood. When she turned the corner, careful not to walk into the oil wall torch she knew was bracketed on the other side, Allie stopped so quickly she nearly fell forward.

"Oh," she said, the smell of food and woodsmoke replaced by the scent of sandalwood.

"My lady," Reid said.

Allie ignored her racing pulse and curtsied, pretending not to notice how different he looked this evening. Clean-shaven and dressed in a rich black surcoat that made his hair appear even lighter, Reid Kerr was even more handsome than usual. Oh, he was the most dangerous sort of man. One who had the ability to rob her of all coherent thought.

When she tried to walk past him, he grasped her arm.

"Going back so quickly?"

She looked down at his hand on the dark fabric of her gown. Large and powerful, like the rest of him. It dropped promptly, and she unaccountably mourned the loss of his touch.

"Gillian will be looking for me," she said without moving.

"Protective," he said.

She remembered what she had told him earlier that day. "Aye, very much so. Especially, it seems . . ." She stopped, wondering how to finish.

Reid did so for her. "About me."

Allie felt every rise and fall of her chest. Though the corridor was empty now, anyone could walk by and see them. And they stood much too close to be proper.

"Aye," she said simply.

Reid looked at her mouth, and she could not resist doing the same with him. What would it feel like if he leaned down and pressed his lips to hers? Allie had been kissed before, once by a man she found quite attractive. Unfortunately, her father had not cared. The match had not been suitably advantageous.

Would it feel the same way with him?

For a wild moment, Allie thought she was about to find out.

"You did well today," he said instead.

Just when she was about to thank him, he added, "For a woman."

Her eyes narrowed.

"What is wrong with you?" she asked sincerely. "Are you utterly incapable of having a conversation without causing insult?"

"It appears not."

"Well then, I congratulate you. If your intent is to make everyone believe you are without sentiment, understanding, or kindness, then you are doing an exceedingly good job."

When that damn smirk appeared, Allie had to resist the desire to stomp on his foot.

"And if you are instead attempting to mask a deep, very well-hidden bit of humanity for some unknown reason," she said, trying not to raise her voice, "then you are quite successful there as well. Either way, I will thank you not to speak to me for the remainder of the evening."

With that, she walked away. Slowing her strides as she neared the entrance of the hall, Allie had to remind herself not to appear angry. The last thing she wished to do was explain herself to Gillian or Aidan. And at the moment, she was not inclined to speak to anyone about the arrogant, insufferable Scotsman, who would unfortunately be training her the next day.

Nay. She would not meet him. If Allie wanted to be insulted, she would go back home to England, to her father. How could she have thought there was any decency in him? She was always too easily swayed, but this time she would learn her lesson.

For the remainder of the evening, and until the council was over, Allie would pretend Reid Kerr did not exist.

8

Allie might not want to train with Reid, but that did not mean she did not wish to train at all.

After a long morning of introduction to the various visiting chiefs, and the Lord Warden himself, she made her excuses and her escape. The timing was perfect—the men's training had been cancelled for the day in favor of a daylong feast and celebration that would not end until darkness fell and supper turned to dinner. It would seem the Lord Warden had arrived just in time. According to Gill, disagreements had begun to turn into arguments. All agreed there was a problem, but none could come to terms on a solution. They needed the fierce man's input and experience. To Allie, the celebrations meant one thing: no one would be roaming around. No one would find her practicing. After pleading a headache, she hurried to her chamber to change into her shirt and stockings, then snuck out the side door of the tower, which led directly to the gatehouse. When Lawrence handed her the sword, she thanked him and made her way down the hill.

Though Allie had considered telling Aidan about her argument with Reid, she'd decided to train alone instead. Her brother-in-law would not be pleased with the risk she took, but she could not bear to sit idle, even on such an overcast day. Much like yesterday, a mist blanketed everything around her, the gray sky not allowing for any glimpses of the sun.

Moving into position, Allie began the session just as Aidan had instructed her to do. Left foot forward, arms at shoulder height. She swung the sword and pulled back, feeling more and more at ease with each movement.

"Remember to bend your back leg."

She swung around and groaned. "No," she said, dropping the sword to her side. How unfair was it for her heart to always beat so rapidly for a man she should hate? "I did not invite you here for a reason."

There it was again.

For the second time since they'd met, his cocksure grin was replaced by an almost sorrowful expression. As he moved toward her, the mischievous twinkle in his eyes was replaced with an honesty she found hard to ignore.

"I did not come here to train you," he said. "I am here to apologize."

Even the tone of his voice was different. He sounded . . . normal. Less sure of himself.

Yet she had vowed to stay away from him. Was she so fickle that one kind word could draw her to him?

Nay!

"Then say the words and be gone."

But he didn't say anything at all. Reid looked at her for so long that Allie felt the need to speak. "Why do you look at me like that?"

"I'm sorry," Reid said finally.

That was it? His grand apology was all of two words?

"Very well. You're sorry." She turned away, willing him to leave, despising herself for wanting him to stay.

"I don't know why I said you only did well for a woman. I meant to say you did well, as well as any man."

She frowned. "Which means much the same."

Allie didn't move. And she most especially did not turn around.

"My sister," he said quietly as the mist continued to gather, "is more capable than most men, and as you know, my sister-in-law wears men's breeches. It's said the woman with whom my brother-in-law fosters can shoot a bow and arrow better than her husband."

Allie did turn back then. "Neill fosters with a woman?"

She had heard plenty about Sara's brother-in-law Neill, a celebrated knight, but certainly not that.

"Nay," he said, still so serious. "He fosters with Sir Adam Dayne, who was once a ward of Sara's late father. They say his wife, Cora, is as skilled as any man, mayhap more so, with the longbow."

Allie's eyes widened. "Truly?"

"Aye," he said. "Truly."

Allie had never seen a woman shoot a longbow before. How did she have the strength to manage such a feat?

"Why?" The question came out before she could help herself.

Reid shrugged. "Likely for the same reason you yourself wield that sword."

He didn't ask, and she did not offer an explanation. At times she thought herself silly for standing here holding a sword and pretending to fight. She wasn't ready to put words to the urge that sent her out here day after day, but she did have a question of her own.

"I meant, why would you say that last eve?"

Again, silence. Finally, he sighed and said, "To push you away."

Allie had not been expecting that.

"Why," she asked, aware of the dangers of such a conversation, "do you wish to push me away?"

"I—" Reid suddenly looked up to the sky, as if such a thing were necessary, to confirm what Allie had long since suspected. It was going to rain at any moment.

"We should go," he said, looking back at her.

Too late. The sky opened up so quickly, there was little time to consider their options for shelter. They could climb the hill back toward the keep, be soaked for the efforts, or . . .

An abandoned dovecote stood between the castle and the clearing, just on the other side of the thicket of trees.

She ran, not looking back to see if he was following.

REID LEANED PAST HER, reaching forward to open the cracked wooden door. Once they were both inside, he looked around with interest. The circular stone structure was still structurally sound, though it clearly had not been used in some time. Hundreds of nesting holes stood empty.

"Why was this abandoned?" he asked.

Allie looked up, shaking her head. "I only know this was built away from the trees, away from birds of prey, and that it was once used to house doves."

He'd assumed as much. They stood, wet and silent, listening to the steady rain outside.

"As soon as it slows down, we'll return to the keep," Allie said, watching him. "So?" she pressed.

She was waiting for him to finish answering her question.

"I thought perhaps you'd forgotten," he said.

Though she didn't smile, exactly, Allie's lips turned up ever so slightly. She reached back to grab the length of her wet hair and pulled it over her shoulder. Reid watched, mesmerized, as she braided it. Her wet linen shirt clung to every curve now, as snug and revealing as the leggings underneath.

"And I thought perhaps you were being sincere?" she said, noticing his

perusal.

He looked into her accusatory eyes. "Is it not possible that I am both sincere and appreciative?"

She rolled her eyes. "You are incorrigible."

"I pushed you away because this is dangerous."

"This?"

"Aye." He gestured to the space between them. "*This.*"

When she pulled her bottom lip into her mouth, biting down gently, Reid should have wanted to bite that same lip and then taste it with his tongue. With any other woman, it would have been the only thought on his mind.

Instead, he found himself wondering about other things. What did she cherish most? How long did she intend to stay here in Scotland? Would she wish to stay?

God's blood, Reid.

"Do you miss your home?" he blurted, attempting to steer his thoughts away from such ruminations. As he awaited her answer, he leaned back against the cold stone wall, putting necessary distance between them.

Allie appeared startled by the abrupt change in topic. "I . . ."

That lip again.

"I do, at times. I miss the people, mostly."

He should not care if Lady Allie wanted to go back.

"But Scotland is my home now."

Pride, joy, relief flooded his senses. He longed to reach for her, but he dug his fingers into the stones behind him instead.

"You said this is dangerous? How so?" she asked, clearly not understanding.

He could easily show her, though he should not. And yet . . . he'd never had much self-control. Ignoring the warnings of his inner voice, he closed the distance between them.

"Because I'm going to kiss you."

He'd never uttered such a warning in his life. But this was different.

She was different.

When his hand touched her cheek, Reid nearly pulled back. What he was about to do was irreversible. This was no simple kiss, and he knew it. But the look she gave him . . . it was his undoing. He moved closer, closing the space between them.

He ran his thumb along the smooth curve of her bottom lip toward the corner of her mouth. He tugged ever so gently, and when her lips parted for him, Reid leaned close and pressed his own lips against those full, pink curves.

Sweet. Soft. Untried.

He tugged his thumb a bit more, using his tongue to show her how to open for him. When she did, Reid groaned, deepening the kiss. He willed her tongue to meet his and cursed himself when it did. She'd accused him of being incorrigible, and she was right.

Reid could never have such a woman, and yet he continued.

Moving his hand from her cheek to the nape of her neck, Reid tugged her closer, until he could feel the press of her breasts against his chest—until he hardened past the point of logical thought. Could she feel his need against her or was she too innocent to understand?

Very much an innocent.

Graeme had said that about her. He'd best remember it.

Reid pulled himself away, resisting the siren's call of her lips, now swollen from his kiss.

Every hair on his body stood on end. As rain pounded the roof above them, Reid closed his eyes and pulled her into his arms. Allie wrapped her hands around his back. He took a deep breath, inhaling the scent of roses mixed with something else. Cloves, nutmeg? He'd never smelled such a scent before.

He'd never held a woman like this before.

How long they stood there, Reid could not be sure. But as the rain slowed, their time together ending, he pulled away.

She looked confused. Understandably so.

"Dangerous," he warned. "As I said."

"And yet you did not push me away today."

"I should have." Reid forced himself to drop his hands and step away. "I'm not the man for you, Allie."

She lifted her chin in defiance. "Then why did you kiss me?"

"Because I wanted to," he said. God, he'd wanted that and so much more. He'd wanted things he had no right wanting.

"I came to apologize," he continued, "but it seems I've only given myself more to apologize for."

"No," she said. "I will not accept that second apology. We've done nothing wrong here."

He laughed, the sound hollow to his own ears. "Nothing wrong? You are unmarried—"

"Would it be more acceptable if I were?" she asked, raising her eyebrows.

"The sister of my host—"

"And a willing participant."

"This was a mistake." Reid turned to leave. "I will tell Aidan you are down here," he said in an attempt to ensure her safety. He did not like the thought of leaving her out here alone, but they couldn't be seen walking back toward the keep together.

He grabbed the iron handle on the door and pulled. Just when he was about to step outside, Allie's voice stopped him.

"I will meet you tomorrow, before the sun sets."

He turned and wished he had not. "Nay, Allie. I cannot—"

"You offered to train me," she said, neither her voice nor expression offering any hint of her feelings. It seemed she had taken his previous day's lesson to heart, much to his current discomfort.

"That was before—"

"You offered, and I accepted. Do you always break your agreements so easily?"

No, he did not. "Very well," he said. "We will meet tomorrow. To train."

When she smiled, Reid knew he had already lost his uncharacteristic battle with self-control. Nay, he'd lost it well before he'd agreed to meet her again. The question was, could Allie help him be found?

9

"How can Graeme pretend all is well?" Allie asked.

She stood with Gillian in the great hall, the meal having long since concluded. An uninformed visitor to Highgate End might comment on the way the trestle tables had been moved to the sides of the room, as they were after each meal, providing a space for socializing and dancing. Or maybe they would admire the music or the array of different colors. With so many guests, it felt as if every color were represented. Allie herself wore a dark lilac gown with two gold clasps and a cream-patterned surcoat.

What an uninformed visitor likely would *not* notice were the undercurrents that had been brewing since the Lord Warden's arrival two days prior. According to Reid, the meetings had continued to be fractious. The warden had not settled matters as they'd hoped.

Careful not to glance her trainer's way, Allie looked to her sister for an answer.

"He is quite good at hosting."

Allie followed Gillian's gaze to her husband, who stood in the center of a group of men that included Douglas. Calm prevailed at the moment, an impressive accomplishment considering what she'd heard about the proceedings.

"Aye," she agreed, "as are you, Gill."

And she meant it. Hosting over fifty guests for nigh a fortnight was no small task, and their mother had never shown much of an interest in training either of them to run a household. "I am so happy for you," she continued. "Who could have imagined a kiss in Kenshire's garden would have led to this."

"Allie, shhh." Gillian's tone was light despite her admonition.

When the musicians began a lilting ballad, Allie stopped teasing her sister to listen. The lyrics were about Thomas the Rhymer. "Isn't he the one who was carried off by the Queen of Elfland and returned with the gift of prophecy?"

Gillian squinted as if it would help her listen. The hall had quieted considerably, but the gathering was large enough, and loud enough, that it was difficult to hear each word. "I believe so."

They did not talk for the remainder of the ballad, and when it was finished, Allie joined in the applause. When the flutist next to the singer began to play the next song, the few women in attendance began to pair with their husbands. As the only unmarried noblewoman in attendance, Allie expected she would be asked to dance, just as she had been the two previous evenings.

"Why the frown?" Gillian asked. "You've always enjoyed dancing."

Allie looked into her sister's eyes. She wished she could confide in her as she'd always done in the past, but Gillian would certainly not sympathize with her problem. In fact, she would be very happy to learn that her suspicions about Reid had come to naught.

Despite the connection they'd shared that day in the dovecote, Reid had mostly ignored her. He no longer looked her way at meals, and though he had continued to train her, he'd spoken of nothing beyond her stance and her longsword.

"Aye, and I still do. Just not this eve."

"I'm sorry to hear it."

Both she and Allie spun around to find Reid watching them intently. Where had he come from?

"I would ask for this dance." His eyes narrowed as if he expected her to decline.

She was not surprised by her body's response, the warmth that flooded her a further testament that, as much as she claimed to dislike Reid Kerr, there was a part of her that did not. When they'd first met, she would have focused on his slight smirk and the arrogant way he wore his good looks. Now, she saw beyond it, into eyes that pleaded for her to accept.

"A shame," Gillian said, her voice cool. Unwelcoming. "My sister—"

"Would be pleased to dance," she said, risking her sister's ire.

Gill gave her a look that required no interpretation, but Allie took his arm anyway, attempting to ignore the fire that ignited in her gut and spread to every limb of her body.

He spun her toward the middle of the dancers, away from her sister's watchful eyes. "Why do you do that?" she asked.

"Do what?"

Allie raised her brows. "Attempt to make others dislike you so."

"Others? You mean your sister? I can assure you, she disliked me well enough before today."

"You don't care?"

His mask was firmly in place once more. "Her opinions are her own."

That was hardly an answer to her question.

They swayed to the music, back and forth across the newly replaced rushes. The great hall had never looked as spectacular as it did tonight, and even though the reason for the gathering was anything but joyous, Scots seemed to welcome any cause to eat, drink, and dance. It was one of the things she loved most about her new home.

"I was taken aback that you asked me to dance."

When she looked up, Allie caught Reid gazing at her lips. It was the first time he'd looked at her like this since their afternoon in the dovecote.

"A moment of weakness," he answered.

Allie pretended not to understand. "Weakness? A dance? Surely a man who can handle the longsword like you has very few weaknesses."

Though she teased him, Reid did not smile. The tick in his jaw made her want to reach up and smooth it away, feel his skin beneath her fingertips.

"As it happens, I do."

He spoke of *her*.

"Then why pretend otherwise these last two days?"

Much to their mother's chagrin and their father's disappointment, Allie had never excelled at playing the part of a compliant young lady. Everyone around her knew her thoughts nearly the same moment as she had them—and yet she had never said anything so bold before.

He spun her around, and unfortunately, Allie met her sister's gaze when he did. Gillian was talking furiously to Graeme, and they were both watching them dance.

"My sister and Graeme are watching," she whispered.

Reid did not look their way. Instead, he spun her once again, surprising her with his dancing skills. "The precise reason why I've 'pretended otherwise,' as you say."

"I don't believe you."

The song was coming to an end much too soon.

"We've been alone on a few occasions—"

"Allie." He spoke so softly she had to watch his lips to be sure he'd spoken. "You don't understand. You don't know me. I am—"

When he stopped, Allie finished for him. "More than you present to the world."

His eyes widened, the mask dropping again. She'd managed to surprise him.

"Pardon me," a voice cut in.

Aidan.

"If I may?"

The song had ended and another had begun. Aidan's outstretched hand waited for her to take it, which of course she was forced to do. It didn't matter that she was not ready.

"Of course," Reid said, handing her over. "I trust in your ability to entertain the lady."

With that, he turned and walked away. She watched as he left the hall, his habitual arrogance wrapping around him again like a well-worn cloak.

"Is all well?"

Nay, it was not, but she forced a smile.

"Aye, Aidan. All is well."

"THE GREAT REID KERR, standing in the shadows."

Reid watched Douglas approach, knowing there was nothing he could do to dissuade the man. He should have left the hall, but he'd made a crucial mistake. Before exiting, he'd turned back to take one last glance at the woman who had so thoroughly entranced him. Now he could not bring himself to retire. Instead, he tormented himself by watching her banter so easily with Aidan de Sowlis.

"Always," he said, accepting the mug of ale Douglas offered.

"You were quiet today."

"I made my clan's position clear."

"Reid." Douglas took a swig of ale. "If we do not accept Caxton's appointment—"

"We will never have peace with that man as the English warden," Reid said, watching as Aidan leaned much too close to Allie.

Douglas sighed. "I dislike the appointment as much as you do, but until we have just cause to appeal to the English king—"

"And if he frees the reivers who attempted to kill my brother? It would be chaos, and you know it." Reid respected the man, as did his brothers, but in this they could not agree.

"I told you, the king knows of the attack on your brother, and he has demanded that we do nothing aside from bringing them to trial at the next Day of Truce. What can we do without the support of our own sovereign?"

"Forgive me, Douglas, if I've lost faith in a system that has set more than one murderer free in the past months. The stakes for Clan Kerr are high."

He risked the warden's ire, but Toren and Reid agreed on this . . . their position would remain firm. Aye, they wanted peace. The Day of Truce had served both countries well for more than thirty years. But the tide was turning, and too many guilty parties had been set free even before Caxton's appointment.

"Your family's alliance with the Waryns—"

"More than an alliance," Reid said. "They are family now."

Douglas grunted. "And yet you talk of a border war."

"Nay, not war—"

"What do you think will happen if we countermand our own king? If we break the Day of Truce?"

Finally, the song was over. Douglas kept talking, but Allie had grabbed his attention once more. Her eyes had shifted from her dancing partner and were darting all around the hall.

Could she be looking for him?

He forced himself to return his attention to Douglas. "If Alexander will not speak to the English king," he began, "then allow a contingency—"

"Nay," Douglas said, his voice firm. "I will not, and well you know it."

Reid drank as both men fell silent. While some of the chiefs agreed with Douglas, they'd all witnessed the increase in raids.

There was no denying the audacity of the English reivers was growing, a situation that would undoubtedly worsen under the new warden.

"If the clans decide to boycott the Day of Truce—"

"That will not happen. Not yet." Douglas stood up straighter. "Clan Kerr will not be swayed?"

Reid looked the warden directly in the eyes. "Nay, we will not."

That both men wanted the same thing hardly mattered.

"Alex—"

"Does not speak for Toren."

Would Douglas have questioned his brother this way?

Nay, likely not, but Reid could hardly blame him. He had not gone out of his way to try earning the man's respect.

"Then who will?"

Douglas was asking not about this council but about the future of Clan Kerr. A subject he did not care to discuss. He would have said as much, except this was Douglas, and no one, not even his brothers, would dare ignore a question from this man.

"Toren has not yet named a second."

Allie stood with Lady Gillian, who seemed to be upset, though no less so than her sister.

"Some say you are not interested."

Reid had wondered how long it would take him to ask. "I am not."

He waited for more questions.

Why are you not interested? What does Toren think of your decision? Who will be named his second?

But they never came. Instead, Douglas looked at him as his father might have done were he alive, with a combination of surprise and censure. He said only, "You would do well in the position."

Reid ignored the comment and instead took his own advice, clearing his expression of emotion, and continued to watch Allie and Gillian's argument.

"To think she could have married Covington," Douglas observed. Though he spoke of Gillian, the same could be said for Allie. What father would promise not one, but two, of his daughters to such a man? They were fortunate to have escaped that sentence.

"They say the father has come back to our side."

"According to Graeme, he only entertained the Earl of Covington to save Lyndwood. As a longtime friend to Kenshire, he must wish for peace as we do." Douglas made a sound that told Reid he was not fully convinced.

"You know as well as I do," Reid said, "allegiances are sometimes complicated."

Again, Douglas did not hide his displeasure. "For some, perhaps. We shall speak more tomorrow." With that, he nodded and walked away.

Reid himself was about to leave when Allie spun away from her sister and fled. It only took him a moment to recover before following her.

And sealing his fate.

10

"Allie?"

Reid thought he had seen her go this way, but she was nowhere to be found. He searched the inner courtyard, walked past a vegetable garden, and stood in the center of the vast, open space, unsure how he could have missed her.

There.

She was halfway up a set of stairs that led to the battlement near the gatehouse when he felt something at his feet. Looking down, he knew his Englishwoman would have to wait. Reid picked up the kitten, pushing back early memories of his mother who refused to allow an animal to go unloved, and placed her so close to his face their noses touched.

"You have no owner," he told her, the grays and browns of her fur melding together like a seamless patchwork. "And are a jumpy one." Though she tried to get out of his grasp, Reid held her a moment longer.

"White paws." *The mark of an angel.* He smiled remembering his father's reaction to that particular assertation made by the woman he'd thought abandoned him. "Well, my wee angel, hear me well. Take what you're offered."

Still now, he had no idea what the words meant. But his mother had uttered them often enough, and inexplicably, all manner of animals returned to her for the nourishment they needed to survive.

With a final rub just beneath her head, Reid put the kitten down and said a silent prayer she would heed his words . . . and live.

When he looked up, Reid called louder to Allie this time. But it seemed there had been no need. She'd already been looking down at him.

"I can't—"

"You are upset."

He always knew what to say, how to say it, and was never at a loss for words.

A guard moved from his position, heading toward them, but he stopped when Allie shook her head.

"Will you walk with me?" He sounded like one of his damn brothers. Maybe even like Catrina's proper English husband. But Reid refused to leave her.

"That depends."

"On?"

"Which Reid is asking?"

He frowned. "There is only one."

"Nay." She shook her head. "There is not. And I do not have patience this eve to spar with the one my sister met at The Wild Boar. The one I met on his first night at Highgate End."

So it was as he suspected. Allie's fight with Gillian had been about him.

"I can be whomever the lady wishes." He said it jokingly, but Allie did not laugh. But she did pick up the hem of her gown and walk back down the stairs.

"Walk with me," he repeated. Offering his elbow in a courtly gesture he'd seen but never had use for before, Reid led Allie back toward the inner gate. When he turned into the grassy area along the walls, Allie did not protest. With only two entrances leading from the outer bailey back toward the keep, they would not separate for at least half of the distance of Highgate Castle.

The sky, lit only by the light of the moon and the torches punctuating the tops of both walls, was at least clear this eve. Reid remained silent, waiting.

"She forbade me to speak to you."

Reid was not surprised. "Yet here we are."

Her arm fit perfectly in the crook of his elbow. Despite her ominous words, Reid was very much enjoying their simple walk.

"She means well," Allie said. "Gillian is accustomed to playing the role of my mother."

"You say that as if your own mother does not play her role well."

She looked at him as if asking a silent question.

Though he rarely talked about his own mother, Reid did not hesitate. "As I'm sure you know, the story of my own is complicated. For many years we thought she abandoned my siblings and I, but we learned just recently she tried only to protect us."

"I had heard she was found and returned to Scotland."

The pang in his chest every time he thought of the mother he hated for leaving, the one they'd been reunited with now living with his brother . . .

"Aye," he said, wanting to tell her more, to explain how her leaving just after his father died had affected him. But instead, he brought them back to her own observation of Gillian's role. "And your own mother? Is she not the nurturing kind?"

Allie's laugh usually lit up everything around her, but this time it sounded bitter. "Nurturing, indeed. She bows to her husband in all things, even when they are wrong."

"Covington?"

It was nearly as quiet here as in the woods where they trained. Reid would have to remember this spot . . . finding privacy in any castle was a difficult feat to accomplish, but he'd had occasion to practice.

"Covington, our tutoring, his insistence Gillian and I should be sheltered at all times. Do you know I have never been to a tournament?"

"Graeme mentioned that you had been sheltered—"

"Father would allow visits only to Kenshire, and my sister was permitted to go more often than I was. 'Reivers,' he would say. 'Dangers everywhere.'"

"He is not wrong."

"Were you able to leave Brockburg?"

She already knew the answer, but he gave one anyway. "We were actually raised at Dunmure Tower and only moved to Brockburg later. But aye, lass, I was able to leave. I also had been trained—"

"Nay, please do not," she said. "I already know your arguments. I've heard them many times over the years."

Reid tried to imagine what it would have been like growing up in one place and never leaving. The very thought pressed in on him. "Did you try?"

Her sigh was one of frustration, of longing, and of lost opportunities.

"I'm sorry," he said, pulling her to a stop.

"You were not there. Why are you sorry for—"

"Not for your upbringing," he said, knowing his next words would change everything. Somehow that knowledge didn't stop him from speaking them. It was as if he were no longer in control of himself. "I'm sorry your sister dislikes me."

Her perfectly arched brows lifted.

"I know I can be hard to . . . like."

"Nay, you are not hard to like at all. Not *this* Reid."

"Allie, there is only *one* Reid. Both are a part of me, and as such I could never be good enough to deserve you. I tried to tell you precisely that earlier today. This is why I've attempted to distance myself from you, why I should not have asked you to dance earlier, and why I should most definitely not be with you now."

She should reject him. Hell, he would reject himself.

"What are you saying?"

If he were a clever man, he would not answer that question. He would do everything in his power to forget this conversation, forget Allie, and ignore her until the council was over.

But he could not.

She had enchanted him. He was drawn to her warmness and enthusiasm, drawn to her bravery and honesty, drawn to everything he was not. And as despicable as he might be, Reid would not dishonor his brothers or his clan, which left him with one choice.

A choice he'd never thought to make.

"I'm asking you if you will accept both sides of me."

Either she was not as surprised as he would have expected, or his lessons on concealing emotion had been shockingly effective. "Accept?"

"I want to kiss you again," he started. "But I'd like to do much more than that. I would feel your every curve beneath my hands, make you mine right here if such a thing were possible."

Her eyes widened.

"I want to be the only man to train you. To dance with you. And I know we've only just met. But I—"

"Aye, Reid. I will marry you."

GILLIAN WAS RIGHT. Allie was not thinking clearly. At least, she must not have been since there was no other explanation for the words that just escaped her lips.

Reid Kerr was the very last man she would have imagined as her husband. He was rude and arrogant, the kind of man who pretended not to care when his actions indicated otherwise.

Oddly enough, it was Aidan who had helped her get to know him. The moment he'd agreed to allow Reid to take over her training, she'd been forced to see the man in a different light.

She didn't know much about love, never having experienced it for a man before, but she'd run from the hall earlier after her sister had said, "He cannot leave Highgate soon enough." She'd been upset with her sister, but it had also struck her that she might never see Reid Kerr again after the council ended.

The thought had filled her with emptiness, along with the knowledge that, once again, what she wanted did not matter . . .

And then he was there.

"You will?"

Oh God, was that not what he had meant? "I thought . . . when you said . . . did you mean—"

"Aye! I did . . . I do want that." He grasped her by both cheeks and forced her to look at him. "But you still don't understand."

"I do," she said. "And my answer remains the same."

His expression softened. "You are too good—"

"Stop," she said. "If your intent is to dissuade me, know that I can be quite stubborn."

His smile elicited a tingling in her very core, a need to touch him back.

She covered his hands with her own. "You said you wanted to kiss me again."

Reid groaned.

"So why don't you—"

His lips came down on hers more firmly than before. This time, she opened for him immediately and was rewarded with an enveloping of warmth, as if she'd just stepped from a cold winter's day directly into summer. His tongue swept inside, and when she touched it with her own, the sound he made burned a path straight to her soul.

Allie wanted to move closer, to feel him against her. Reid tilted his head, his lips seemingly everywhere at once. When he wrapped his arms around her, pulling her closer, Allie did the same with him. Their kiss consumed her, and she never wanted it to end.

"If we don't stop," he murmured, breaking away, "I will take you here in full view of him."

It took a moment for Allie to understand. She followed his gaze up, and sure enough, a guard stood atop the outer wall, watching them. Though he immediately looked away, Allie moved back from Reid.

"He saw us!"

The corner of his mouth lifted ever so slightly. "So he did."

Reid pulled her back toward him. Lifting her hair ever so gently from her shoulder, he leaned in and placed a kiss on her neck.

"But . . ." She tried to look up. "Should we—"

"Find a more private place? Aye, but only if you're willing to relinquish your virginity this very night."

Was he jesting? Allie pulled back. "Surely you don't mean—"

Reid cocked his head to the side. "Go on."

She would never reference such a thing out loud. Allie was bolder than her sister, but she was not *that* bold. "I just meant . . . you are indelicate."

He did not disagree with her. Indeed, he nodded.

"And arrogant."

Another nod.

"And—"

"Enamored," he said. "Enthralled, enchanted, and bewildered by my own actions."

He could be charming when it served him too, but Allie would not mention that. He already knew.

"What shall we do now?" she asked.

His slow smile told her he'd deliberately misunderstood.

"If you're willing to ignore our curious friend, I can initiate you to a world of pleasure."

"I meant"—and he knew this—"about us."

Reid turned serious then, and she hated being responsible for that. But there were many obstacles for them still, including her own sister.

"Gillian forbade me to speak to you," she added. "I hardly think she will agree to give her blessing to our marriage."

Saying it aloud dampened her mood at once, but it did not shake her certainty. Allie hardly knew Reid, and a few days before she would have gladly tossed him into the moat . . . if Highgate had one. And yet, no one had ever before seemed to fit her the way he did. No, she had no doubts about her hasty decision. The idea of seeing him leave Highgate, never to return, made her feel as if the bottom of her stomach had dropped out.

"You do not need her blessing."

"She is my sister. And in the absence of my father—"

"Allie." Reid took her hand. "You need no one. We could hand-fast now. Or be married any time by simply saying the words."

Though his words were, indeed, true, she could not do something like that behind Gillian's back, knowing she did not approve. She tried to make him understand in a different way. "What if your brothers did not like me?"

He shrugged. "That would not matter, lass."

"You would marry me even if Toren asked you to do otherwise?"

"He is married to an Englishwoman, as is my brother Alex."

"Nay," she said, squeezing his hand, willing him to understand. "I meant to say, if Toren asked you not to marry me—"

"I would ignore him."

"And if he asked as your chief?"

Reid's eyes narrowed. "He'd never do such a thing."

"Forget your brothers." She frowned, pushing away from him with a prickling of doubt. "I want Gillian to like you."

He was clearly not convinced, his arms shutting her out, folded in front of him.

"I want her to see you as I do. And for our families to have the kind of relationship you have with the Waryns. If not with Lyndwood, then with my sister at least. And Clan Scott."

Reid scowled, his brows furrowing together. "You mean the kind of relationship you have with Aidan?"

What was his problem?

"Precisely!" she said, putting more emphasis on the word than was necessary.

And then she understood the source of his distress. He was not the only one who'd misjudged her relationship with Aidan. Others had made similar comments. She should not like that he was jealous of her brother-in-law, but a small part of her smiled inside.

"Reid, he is like a brother to me. He's called me sister from the start. Aidan showed both Gillian and me kindness when we knew no one here."

"I do not leave Highgate End without you."

When he pulled her toward him once again, Allie breathed in his scent, still so unfamiliar to her, as was the man himself. Everything about this made no sense. She'd never been this rash before, nor had she intended to marry so soon. Indeed, she'd hidden here in Highgate End to avoid her father's matchmaking. She'd wanted simple happiness here in Scotland, a reprieve from her staid life in Lyndwood.

There was nothing simple about the man whose arms were wrapped around her, the one she'd unbelievably agreed to marry. Yet she would not let him go. He needed her, and somehow she knew they would be right together. "Then you will just have to charm her as you did me."

"That, my little lass," he said, tucking her head against his chest, "I can do easily enough."

11

*R*eid was going to strangle Lady Gillian.

He'd spent the past two days attempting to speak to her, but it seemed his past transgressions would not allow for an opening. If Allie considered herself stubborn, she was entirely compliant compared with her sister.

Gillian simply did not like him.

He knew he'd acted like a bit of an arse when they first met. He'd been annoyed at her now-husband for his lack of action against English raiders. It was de Sowlis land that had been raided, after all, and an innocent woman had lost her life. He would have preferred for Graeme to react more strongly, though he should have expected the clan chief's tempered response. It was the way the man approached everything.

Reid was brought back to the present—yet another meeting with the Lord Warden and the border chiefs—when a bout of screaming ended with Douglas slamming his fist on the table and the chief of Clan MacDuff threatening to leave before they reached an accord. Someone called for a break, and Reid used it as an opportunity to seek out the lady of Highgate Castle. He found her just outside the kitchen on the path toward the great keep, where the evening meal was already being prepared.

"Lady Gillian, a word?"

When she turned to look at him, her resemblance to Allie caught him off guard. He didn't always see it, and not just because Gillian had freckles whereas her sister did not. They carried themselves so differently—while Gillian had the carriage of a proper lady, the kind who cared about appearances and would never, ever consider fighting with a longsword, Allie was much freer in her movements. More spirited.

"I'm sorry," she said, walking past him. "There is much to be done before the—"

"I've offended you."

It was not a question, and they both knew it.

When Gillian stopped and looked at him, as if cataloguing his flaws, he felt less confident that he'd be able to make good on his promise to Allie. This was the first time Gillian had acknowledged him directly since the start of the council, and Reid almost wished she had not done so.

"I apologize for the first evening we met, at The Wild Boar."

"Apology accepted." Her tone told him just the opposite. With those few curt words, she turned her back to him and walked away.

He thought about going after her, but decided to wait until the meal.

Someone whistled. "I've never seen her quite like this before."

Aidan. He'd just come from the kitchen and had a fresh-baked loaf in his hands.

"Attempting to make amends with Lady Gillian?" He tore off a hunk of bread, a good-natured smile firmly in place, and handed it to him.

Reid accepted the offering.

They stood there for a moment, eating the bread and watching as servants picked herbs and vegetables and visitors wandered the expansive courtyard. It struck Reid that it had been some time since Brockburg Castle had seen this many guests. Lady Juliette had done much to revive a home that had become little more than a place to eat and train after his father's death.

"Attempting, though not succeeding," Reid finally said.

"Why?"

The question startled him.

"I know you, Kerr, and you're not one for idle conversation. Or for caring much for the opinion of others."

Reid feigned surprise. "You wound me, de Sowlis."

The other man would not be so easily deterred. "You did not answer my question."

Nor would he. Reid had agreed to keep his arrangement with Allie a private matter until her sister could be swayed. Which he absolutely needed to do. Although he'd told Allie her family's consent did not matter to him, he had since reconsidered. Clan Scott were their allies, and moreover, de Sowlis and his brother agreed with the Kerrs on how best to handle the current border disputes—by removing the new English warden from his position. He didn't wish to be the one to destroy that.

"It irks me that a woman, any woman, has such a strong reaction to me." Which was, at least, partially true.

"And Allie?"

He could not give up any more information. "Is quite good with the longsword."

"I saw you together two evenings ago."

Outside the castle walls? Had the guard told him? Or—

"Dancing." Aidan finished the last bite of warm bread in his hand, smiling at Reid as if they shared a secret.

Reid was beginning to lose patience with the man's insinuations. "If you have something to say, de Sowlis, say it."

Aidan did not appear to be in a hurry to do so. He took his time chewing, then shrugged. "Very well." Squaring his shoulders, he crossed his arms. "We've had this discussion before, but it seems as if a repetition is warranted. If your intentions with Allie are not honorable—"

"We did have this very discussion."

"Aye, but then I had nothing but a suspicion."

"About?"

"Allie's feelings toward you. As I said before, I know you to be an honorable man—"

"De Sowlis—"

"I've spent quite a bit of time with Allie, as you know. I've seen her in the company of men more powerful and"—Aidan grinned —"much handsomer than you. I have eyes, Kerr, and knew immediately there was something between you. Despite everything . . . I like you. It would be a good match—for you, for Allie, and for our clans."

"You encouraged it by allowing me to train her." Reid should have suspected as much from the start, but he had been too enamored with Allie to question why the man would have given over her training so easily.

"Graeme may not agree, and certainty Gillian does not. She genuinely does not like you."

"But how did you know—"

"Though her words may have said otherwise, the truth of Allie's feelings show whenever she is around you. As I said, I only knew for sure when I saw you dancing in the hall. I can tell you care for her, so the question now is . . . why are you hiding your affection?"

He'd not lie directly to Aidan, his ally, and the man who would be his brother-in-law.

"Lady Gillian."

Aidan waited for him to explain.

"Allie wants her sister to like me—"

A harsh laugh cut him off. "So we will not be allied as family after all."

He ignored that. "And, of course, your brother—"

"Do not worry about Graeme. He knows you as I do."

Precisely the cause for his concern. "And that recommends me to him?"

Aidan clasped his shoulder. "You are not all bad, Kerr. If you were, we would not be having this conversation. Though I will admit, I don't understand your position in the clan. You belong by Toren's side as his—"

"Do not." His voice was low, hard. A warning.

Aidan dropped his hand.

"We were discussing Allie—"

"Who will be a member of your clan," Aidan pointed out.

Reid remained silent, knowing Aidan would not drop the matter.

"When Alex moved to Dunmure, I thought surely—"

"I want it," he spat out, anger and resentment oozing from the words. What the hell was wrong with him? He'd never said those words aloud. First he'd opened his heart to Allie, and now he was unburdening himself to Aidan de Sowlis, a man that had been his enemy once. Or, more precisely, a man whose father had been an enemy to his own. Reid had never taken issue with either de Sowlis brother. He would have dropped the feud long ago, but his brother had remained stubborn, unnecessarily dragging out their clans' enmity.

It took a moment for Aidan to recover, and the look of surprise on his face was keen enough for Reid to regret his words. "Then take it."

He shook his head. "You don't understand."

"You're wrong," Aidan said. "I understand more than most. Do you forget I am the younger brother of Graeme de Sowlis?"

Reid frowned. "Alex was—"

"Toren's second. And you should replace him now," Aidan said, his voice firm.

I could never replace Alex. His brother always makes the right deci-sion and never questions himself.

He could not discuss this now. "Let it go, Aidan."

As they watched, the clan leaders who had ventured outside began to make their way back into the keep.

"It appears another round of shouting and fist pounding is about to commence," he said, not looking forward to the remainder of the afternoon.

"And some hoped this would be over in a matter of days."

Reid glanced back toward the kitchen. "I hope Highgate is prepared for us."

The cost of hosting so many guests for an extended period would be substantial.

"We are prepared," Aidan said as they walked toward the keep. "But, more importantly, are you prepared for Lady Gillian?"

Reid would have said yes once, but he'd begun to doubt everything he thought he knew about himself.

"I am," he lied. "And will do whatever it takes to win her to my side." That was the truth. For Allie, he would do anything.

"I REFUSE."

Allie wanted him to show her more advanced maneuvers, but she simply wasn't ready.

"Do you know how long I've practiced this? Most take years to get this—"

"You are still holding back."

They faced each other, swords drawn, repeating the same movements over and over. Reid understood her frustration, but he would not allow her impatience to get her injured.

"Besides"—he drew back and tossed his sword to the side—"your grip is slipping. If you don't get that right, you cannot advance."

He moved to stand behind her. Though he could just as easily explain what she needed to do, he'd not touched her once this session. Reaching around her waist, he moved her hand lower on the weapon.

"As you swing, your hand continues to slide away from the end of the hilt. Keep it here, like this."

Her hair, always braided during their training, tickled his nose as he leaned closer. He took a deep breath, allowing himself the distraction. "I would wake up every day to this smell."

Allie lowered her sword as he moved his hands to her waist and pulled her to him. When he placed a soft kiss on her neck, she sighed breathily, then said, "Is this part of the training?"

"Hmmm." Reid allowed his hands to move upward, and though he knew how quickly he could lose control, how easily he seemed to do so whenever she was near, he couldn't help himself.

Days had passed since their secret betrothal, and other than their training sessions, he had to make do with quick kisses and exchanged glances. Given the opportunity to touch her at will, Reid was simply not strong enough to resist.

"Your training in this area will be much more . . . intense soon." His hands moved upward, cupping her breasts. The thin material of her shirt was hardly a barrier and very much a threat to his control. "It unfortunately must wait until after the wedding, though I will admit, it will not be an easy task."

Wedding.

He was actually planning to take this woman as his wife. He'd never thought he could look upon such an event with anticipation. Nay, eagerness. If he was scared, it was only because he was most assuredly not worthy of such a woman.

"I don't deserve you," he murmured against her neck.

Planting the tip of the sword into the ground in front of her, Allie gave herself to him completely. She leaned back against him, a soft moan escaping her lips as Reid moved on from her neck, trailing the gentlest of kisses upward.

"You underestimate yourself," she said. The tug in his chest warred with the one against his breeks as he pressed up against her. The sensation of his fully hardened cock making contact with Allie's backside, separated only by a few thin layers of fabric, threatened the promise he'd made to himself.

He had nearly killed his brother-in-law for taking his sister's virginity before they wed—he would not be fool enough to make that same mistake. They could wait.

He could wait.

Or could he?

"Though a wee bit of early training—"

"Allie!"

Reid let go of her so quickly she nearly fell. He'd reached for his sword before he even realized the voice was a woman's.

Gillian's, to be precise.

Allie's sister stood much too close. How had he not heard her approaching? Reid had never been so careless before. He had never seen Gillian look anything but proper, although that might be because he'd never seen her this angry before. Her chest rose and fell with heaving breaths, her eyes flashed at Allie.

"What are you about?" she demanded.

Reid restrained himself from answering, knowing she would not be pleased with any response from him.

"You." Her eyes narrowed. "You are despicable—"

"Nay, Gillian, do not."

"My sister is not some tavern wench you can mishandle, Reid Kerr." She spat his name out as if it were an epithet. "Get away from her."

"Gill," Allie admonished her sister, her hands visibly shaking as she stood by his side. He had the urge to grab her hand and steady it, to let her know that Gillian's words affected him only because they upset her. But he didn't dare.

"What could you have been . . ." Gillian finally looked down toward Allie's other hand "Is that a sword?"

He expected Allie to attempt to explain. To show her sister

some of the fire she so often showed him. Instead, a single tear dropped down her cheek.

Reid hated seeing her so defeated. His Allie was a warrior.

"Allie . . ." He could not allow her to be in such pain without showing her—

"Do not touch her."

He looked back and forth between the sisters. Though he knew Gillian did not care for him, he was surprised by the vehemence of her words. "Lady Gillian, I can assure you—"

"And I can assure you, if you dare lay another hand on my sister, you will no longer be welcome here at Highgate End. Leave us."

He would not engage with Lady Gillian now, but he couldn't bear to leave Allie alone with her.

Allie must have seen the indecision in his eyes.

"I will be fine, Reid. Go," she said.

He hesitated, but this was her sister. Reid reminded himself Gillian was only trying to protect her sister.

He nodded, holding out his hand for the sword, which she gave him. As for Gillian . . . "My lady, we need to discuss—"

"I do not wish to speak with you. Now or ever. Perhaps I did not make myself clear earlier. Or let me say it a bit differently. 'I would not presume to discuss such matters now.'"

It took him a moment to understand, but the mocking tone quickly brought him back to their first meeting. He'd said those words to Graeme at The Wild Boar, not wanting to be overheard by the tavern's patrons. But Lady Gillian had clearly taken it to mean he did not wish to speak openly in front of her, a woman.

"You are mistaken, my lady. I did not mean—"

"Did you mean to take the barmaid to your bed?" she mocked. "Surely I did not mistake your intentions with that woman in The Wild Boar."

Reid tried to remain calm, but she was beginning to provoke him.

"Nay," he said. "You did not." He gripped the hilt of Allie's sword tightly. "I took her to my bed."

Reid heard Allie's gasp behind him as he walked away, and though he was immediately sorry for the hard words, he did not take them back.

Not only had he failed to endear himself to Gillian, but Allie was no doubt furious with him as well. The last thing he heard was Gillian saying, "You have much to explain."

1 2

*A*llie was shaking.

Angry with both her sister and Reid, she sunk deeper into the wooden tub, determined not to get out until the water turned cold. With so many guests in attendance, Allie would not normally have asked for a bath to be brought to her chamber. But she needed time alone. She'd already asked Morgan to bring her meal to her.

Gillian had not been happy, of course, but Allie would not be swayed.

Morgan had left a washing cloth and bar of rose-scented soap on a stool next to the tub. She picked up both items and began to wash, attempting to cleanse away the entire afternoon. The memories clung to her, resistant to her efforts.

She'd tried to explain her training to Gillian, who of course did not understand. More importantly, her sister refused to even discuss the matter of Reid. And when Gillian pointed to his parting words as evidence of the man's character, Allie had not known what to say.

The words had been harsh.

They'd come from the same man who'd propositioned her outside this tower.

The one who looked at others as if they lived to serve his pleasure. The one who did not appear to care about anything or anyone. Who wielded words as weapons just as sharp as the swords with which the men trained.

Reid had said that this man was a part of him, and here was her evidence, but she knew it was not the sum of him.

Aye, as Gillian had been quick to remind her, she *had* been sheltered at Lyndwood. Her sister might be right—she knew little of the world and of men. And yet . . .

I know that Reid looks at me differently than anyone else. And that he cares for me.

"Ahh," she groaned when the door opened behind her. "Not yet, Morgan."

She'd not expected the maid so soon. She must have gone straight to the kitchen, for the meal could not have already begun.

"I've just begun to wash."

"Then allow me to assist you."

Allie spun around so quickly the water splashed all around her and onto the floor.

"Reid! What are you—"

He pulled the stool out next to the tub and sat on it as if he were a king . . . the stool, his throne.

"You cannot . . ." She looked down at the murky water. A white sheen hid all but her shoulders and arms. When Allie glanced back up, the look in Reid's eyes sent a shiver down her spine despite the warmth of the water.

"Your maid said that you did not plan on attending the evening meal."

Allie swallowed. The intensity in his gaze pulled her toward him, gripped her and refused to let go. "I do not."

"Why?"

"What are you doing here?"

"I'm sorry," he said. "For taunting your sister that way."

"Telling her you bedded a tavern maid, you mean?"

He winced.

"You know how I feel about my sister's approval. Why would you say such a thing?"

"Because I was angry."

"You cannot lash out every time someone makes you angry. Will you do that with me?"

Though she was clearly making him uncomfortable, Allie did not relent. "And how will you act when it does not work? When I refuse to be pushed away?"

Reid did not answer.

"We need to make this right." Were they really having this conversation as she sat naked in a tub of water? At least the sheen on top hid her body.

"That's why I am here, Allie. I should not have said what I did, but your sister . . ."

"Is proving stubborn," she said. "But this afternoon changes nothing. We cannot begin our lives together in such a way."

"I know."

Allie could not have been more surprised. "You do?"

"Aye, lass. I understand the bond between siblings. And neither do I want our clans to have a reason to fight each other. We have enough enemies to the south without creating more from former allies."

"What do you propose?"

Allie reached into the water below to look for the soap she'd dropped.

"I will speak to her—"

"Nay, that is not enough." Where was that soap? She hesitated to move around more, lest she disturb the water and reveal all to Reid.

"What else can I do?" he asked.

"Honor her wishes," she said, meeting his eyes. He was not going to like this, but Allie knew her sister. Though she could be quite docile and hesitant, a product of their parents' tutelage, when it came to her, Gillian turned fiercely protective. Until recently, her sister had always obeyed their father in all things. Remain within the castle walls? Gillian did not stray. Marry an old man with a more-than-questionable reputation? Gillian obeyed.

But when she found Allie in the gardens one day crying, begging to go on an adventure—just one—Gillian had risked their father's wrath to take her away from Lyndwood for the day. Despite his forbidding it, they rode well beyond the castle walls to the eastern edge of their property, a spot well-known by all for its beauty. And the moment she learned Allie had been betrothed to that same horrid man, Gillian had left Highgate End in haste in the hopes of stopping it.

If Gillian believed Reid Kerr was bad for her, she would do everything possible to ensure he stayed away. If not for the severity of the situation at the border, he would have likely already been asked to leave Highgate End. But thankfully, doing so would not allow Clan Kerr a voice in what would be a pivotal decision for border relations. Her sister was protective, not foolish.

There was only one way to get her blessing . . .

"Prove to her that you are a man of honor."

"You ask me to honor her wishes . . . what are they?"

Ah, there it was. But the soap was slippery, and as soon as Allie gripped it, the little bar flew back out of her fingers. "That you stay away from me."

As she suspected, Reid was not pleased by the idea. "That will not—"

"Reid, please. Let me speak to her. Give her some time—"

"We do not have time."

"Has there been an agreement between the clans?"

Reid shook his head. "Nay, but the council will not last forever."

"Just a few days," she said. "Give her a chance to become accustomed to the idea, and let me handle her. Before others, act as if you've heeded her words. Deferred to her wishes. Please?"

She had pushed too far. Reid's eyes narrowed and his jaw clenched so tight it had to hurt. She wasn't sure the man was capable of deference.

"Reid?" Abandoning her search for the soap, Allie gripped the cloth underwater and watched Reid's expression soften.

As it always seemed to do with her.

"Very well," he said finally. "We will try this your way." He leaned in toward the tub. "On one condition . . ."

"Anything."

He gripped the side of the tub. When he gave her a wicked smile, Allie knew she'd responded much too quickly.

"Then you won't mind if I recover your soap."

It took her a moment to understand, but by then it was too late. His hand had already slipped into the tub.

"Reid, my maid—"

"Will be quite surprised if she returns now." He paused in his search, and she found she did not want him to stop. "Are we agreed?"

Allie's heart thudded in her chest, though she could not feel his hand. Yet.

"Agreed."

The word no sooner left her lips than she felt the lightest brush of his fingertips along her waist. The taunting touch became more pronounced as those fingers moved along her hip. When his hand continued its exploration and finally settled on her breast, Allie leaned into it as his thumb and forefinger came together to caress her nipple. She could see the top of his hand as it dipped beneath the water and then resurfaced. Mesmerized by the motion, Allie felt an unexpected tingling between her legs.

"I do not believe you will find the soap there," she managed, chancing a glance up at his face.

Allie wished she hadn't done that.

Reid's eyes, hooded and intense, held her own in their thrall. His hand glided down, away from her breast and toward her stomach, as Reid leaned closer toward the tub.

"Is it here, perhaps?" Pretending to search for the errant item, he explored and teased, his hand moving lower still.

"I do not believe so," she said, the words coming out in a strange, throaty voice that sounded unlike her own.

Then he smiled.

Allie sucked in a breath, her heart beating wildly in anticipation of . . . she wasn't sure. She only knew he was planning something.

"Relax," he said.

Allie had thought she was relaxed. In fact, she couldn't ever remember feeling this relaxed before. But when his hand slipped toward her curls, Allie understood. He would touch that most private place. A man who was not yet her husband, who should not be in her bedchamber and should certainly not be touching her.

"Trust me."

She did. It was impossible to account for, the trust she had in this man, but she did trust him. And when his finger dipped even lower, between her legs, she nearly burst out of the tub. "Oh!"

She had not been expecting that.

The smile never left his face, and as Reid moved a finger inside her, she continued to watch him. When she arched up toward his hand, the water moved with them. And though she should probably be considering the consequences of being caught in such a compromising position, Allie concentrated instead on the feel of his strong, powerful hand so delicately caressing her very core.

"Reid, I—"

She spoke even though she had no words.

"I know," he said.

What did he know? What was happening?

She moved her hips to the rhythm he set, slow at first and then faster and faster.

Part of her wanted to close her eyes, but she could not stop looking at Reid's secret smile, the one that told her she was close to something wonderful.

"That's it," he said. "Come for me, sweet Allie."

The words meant nothing.

And everything.

She could no longer control her eyes and they slammed shut just as she tightened and shuddered against him. As she gripped the side of the tub with one hand and his arm with another, Allie's world changed forever. The glorious sensations continued to roll through her until she finally opened her eyes, her heart swelling as warmth spread through her entire body. Reid appeared as pleased to have given her pleasure as she was to be reveling in it.

"Alas," he said. "I do believe your soap is lost forever."

He began to pull his hand away, but when she felt her hip knock against something solid, Allie grabbed it and placed the bar in his hand.

"Perhaps not."

He took it from her and glided it across her waist, her chest. His hand dipped underwater and up again as he traced her body with the soap.

Allie closed her eyes and laid her head back against the tub's rim, giving herself over to Reid completely. Her eyes flew open when a groan—a deep, guttural sound—met her ears.

Pulling his hand out from the tub, Reid offered the soap to her. "More of this, and I will be joining you in there, maid or no."

The thought of Reid bathing alongside her in the small tub made her giggle. "I'm sure you would not fit in here with me."

"Tempt me to find out, and Gillian will find her sister's wedding as hastily planned as her own."

Allie shivered. The thought of being found like this and forcibly wed to Reid was . . . oddly exciting.

"The lady thinks I jest."

Reid flicked his fingers, splashing water on her cheek. She answered with a much larger splash of water that forced him away from the tub.

"I concede," he said, standing. "Will you come down tonight?"

"Nay, I—"

"Not even to see me?" he said, clutching his heart as if she wounded him.

Allie smiled.

"Come," Reid said. "I will not make any advances. But know, when I look at you"—his wicked grin warned her of the naughtiness of his next words—"I will be remembering the feel of you beneath my fingers."

And so it was that she found herself dressing for the meal not long after Reid left her chamber. The power of that man's persuasive skills would lead her to trouble yet.

"Kerr."

Gillian had already warned him away, again, at the entrance to the hall, but it would appear her husband wished to issue another warning as well. Would he have to face the entire household before he took a seat?

"You did not forbid me to speak with her," he said.

"Speak?" Graeme's laugh was not one of joy.

Another man might not have known the man was angry. He appeared calm, his expression neutral, but Reid was not fooled. De Sowlis was furious, just as he'd expected him to be.

"It is my understanding you were not caught *speaking* to her."

Reid wanted to remind the man of the reason he and Gillian were now married, but such a thing would hardly fit Allie's plan. So instead, Reid said nothing.

"I thought we understood each other."

When a maid offered them each a mug, Reid took one from her. It occurred to him belatedly that rather than encouraging Allie to attend the meal, he should have stayed away himself. Though hiding from a fight was not his usual course, he should have allowed the lord and lady of Highgate End time to cool.

"I understood that you did not wish for me to do Lady Allie any injury. And I have no intention to harm her in any way."

Graeme's scowl deepened. "What *are* your intentions, then?"

He'd promised Allie none would know of their agreement until Gillian approved of the match. Keeping that promise would make things more difficult.

"I don't know."

"Not the right answer, Kerr."

He had given his word to de Sowlis as well, and he'd do his best to honor both that and the one of his intended.

"The situation is delicate," he began, aware of Graeme's intense gaze. "But know this as a man of honor. My intentions are pure, my word, unwavering. Lady Allie is an extraordinary woman, and I will do right by her by following her lead in this."

Lady Gillian had arrived at the high table. She watched them from on high, and when her hand lifted, Graeme nodded, taking a step toward the dais. He then turned to Reid one last time.

"I will rely on your reputation as an honorable man, like your brothers, in this. But know well, Reid, if you hurt her, there will be repercussions."

Reid nodded, for he did not intend to do so even knowing, for this night at least, he must distance himself from her.

Until he saw her.

Allie must have entered the hall while he was talking to Graeme. He told himself not to stare, but it was simply not possible. During training, her hair usually hung down her back in a long braid, and at dinner, she wore it piled atop her head or pulled away from her face.

But not tonight.

Allie had not noticed him yet. She was mid-conversation with someone, one of the few wives in attendance, it appeared, but his eyes were only for her. Her hair cascaded down her back, neither straight nor curly. When she reached up to sweep an errant strand from her front shoulder to her back, he almost crossed the room to her.

She reached out to touch the woman's arm, a warm gesture he'd seen her use with other people, though never with him. But now . . . now this gorgeous creature would be his for all time. The thought did not terrify him, and Reid found himself caring less and less about the teasing that would certainly accompany the announcement of their betrothal. Toren and Alex would rightfully have much to say about him taking an English bride after he'd pledged never to take a wife, and certainly not an English one.

One woman, forever.

Reid remembered their interlude in her chamber and imagined a similar scene unfolding at Brockburg in the comfort of their own bedchamber. He grew hard thinking of what would happen next.

She looked at him. And though their eyes only met for the briefest moment, Reid's chest swelled with pleasure. Unfortunately, she was not the only one to pay him any mind. Both Gillian and Graeme were watching him, and neither looked pleased. If he hoped to survive long enough to convince his hosts of his worthiness, he would need to practice greater subtlety.

"You are not doing so well, Kerr."

He groaned . . . another de Sowlis. "If you are here to warn me away—"

"I've already told you that I believe the match is a good one. Why would I warn you away?" Aidan caught the attention of a nearby maid carrying a wooden tray of mugs and raised his hand.

She fairly tripped in her haste to reach them. "A mug of ale, my lord?"

The words were addressed to him, and Reid did not correct the title, though he did ignore the batting of her eyelashes and not-so-subtle advances. "Thank you."

Each of them took a mug, and when nothing more was said, the woman frowned and turned away.

"No longer interested in pretty blonde maids?" Aidan took a swig of ale.

"No," Reid confirmed. And although he had promised Allie to keep quiet about their marriage, he found himself saying, "There will be no others, ever."

When he finally looked at Aidan, the other man was watching him with an unnerving intensity.

"What is it, de Sowlis?"

Aidan raised his mug to him. "A drink," he said.

"To what do we drink?"

"Love."

Whatever Aidan saw on his face made him sputter out a laugh as he swallowed his next mouthful of ale.

"Relax, Kerr," he said. "It's an affliction others have survived. My brother included."

Reid could not help but frown as he looked at that very brother. The man looked back, his expression bleak.

"It may not matter," he said, "if that brother kills me."

Aidan chuckled like a man who was not being targeted for murder.

"You are enjoying this," Reid accused, shifting his gaze to the younger de Sowlis.

"It is much more diverting than the council, you will admit."

Aidan shifted seamlessly to a discussion of the latest council meetings. Reid attempted to listen, but that word caught him up.

Love.

Aye, he *was* in love with her. It was the only explanation for the madness that had shaped these past few days. The only reason he'd decided he needed to take her to wife. But how had he fallen in love in such a short time?

"Do you agree?"

Reid stared blankly back at Aidan.

"I'd ask what, or whom, you're thinking about rather than listening, but I don't believe such a question is necessary."

"I never expected this."

"I doubt any man does."

They both watched as Allie ascended the dais and took her regular seat next to her sister.

"Allie is an easy woman to love," Aidan said knowingly.

"Aye. I will be forever in your debt for what you've done."

"Do not thank me yet." Aidan nodded toward the head table.

Two murderous gazes peered down at Reid.

"If only your reputation were as pristine as mine, you'd have an easier time of it."

Reid's bitter laugh was all too real. "Aye, who'd want their sister to marry the arse of the Kerr family?"

Aidan winked and began to walk away. "I think that description may be a bit too kind," he said, already laughing at his own joke.

Was he really that bad?

***

"Sister."

Allie laughed. "Brother."

She couldn't have been happier to see Aidan. The unusual tension between her and Gillian chafed—enough so that she would have snuck out of the hall had her sister not been so carefully watching her. Though their discussion had not even skirted Reid Kerr, the topic had shadowed everything that was said between them.

She'd seen Reid, of course, though she'd pretended not to.

"You've arrived just in time," Allie said, lifting her goblet to Aidan.

"For what?"

"My soundness of mind."

Though tradition dictated that Aidan should sit on his brother's left, he'd started sitting next to her after they began their training. She had never been more grateful for the arrangement than she was this evening.

They chatted idly for a few moments, Allie straining to ignore the flash of a royal blue surcoat moving from the hall's entrance. Best to let Gillian believe she'd heeded her advice for now, until her sister calmed down enough to act more reasonably.

Then Aidan caught her off guard by saying, "When you first asked me to train you, I wondered if you felt unsafe here. I considered explaining to you that you'd always be safe here, and that arming yourself was not necessary—"

"But you did not." Allie took a deep sip of the French red wine, allowing it to slip down her throat. Where was he going with this?

"Nay. I knew it would not dissuade you. Besides, I began to understand why you wanted it so badly."

"Hmm, that is quite a feat since I hardly understand it myself."

Aidan sighed and looked out into the crowd. She could not allow her gaze to follow his, though she felt certain he was staring at a certain rogue in a blue surcoat.

"You wanted adventure but were told to remain inside Lyndwood—"

"For my own protection," she whispered, repeating what she'd been told over and over again.

"You wanted your sister to be happy, but your father promised her to Covington."

Allie swallowed. "So we would not lose Lyndwood."

"You wanted to learn the healing arts, but your parents would not allow it."

Allie placed her goblet back onto the table. "It was not necessary for me to do so. We had a healer already—"

"And you wanted to learn to train with the longsword. I figured I could at least give you that—just one of the things you wanted." He paused, staring at her intently. "And now there is something else that you want," he whispered. "And I will help you get that too."

This time, she did look into the crowd. And when her eyes met Reid's, she nearly lost control. The look on his face . . . she would never forget it. He wanted her. Nay, it was more than that. He *needed* her.

"Why?" she asked, turning back. "Why have you always been so kind to me, Aidan?"

His smile was so kind, so loving. She marveled over how accepted this man had made her feel, right from the beginning of her time at Highgate.

"Because there is something I want too."

She sniffled, trying to hold back tears.

"What? What do you want, Aidan?" She would give him anything.

But he did not answer, so she repeated her question, more loudly this time.

"A sister," Graeme said. "He wants a sister. And always has."

When she turned back to Aidan, he was smiling.

"Of course," she said at once. "I've thought of you as a brother from the moment I arrived here. I couldn't be more honored."

Aidan hid his face behind his mug and finally finished it with a long swig. "Understand, Allie, that I will always, always protect you and love you, as only a brother can do."

Allie wiped away the single tear that escaped from the corner of her eye. The acceptance and love she and Gillian had found here was beyond belief. It was nothing like the relationship they had with their parents.

"As will I," Gillian added, the resolve in her voice unmistakable.

Allie looked from Aidan to Gillian, and though she wasn't sure how much her sister had overheard of their conversation, one thing was for sure.

They had a long few days ahead of them.

"War has been declared."

Allie's eyes widened. Aidan had found her in Wern Hall, a much smaller—and infinitely more private—version of the great hall. Accessible only through a secret passageway from the kitchen, it was one of the very few places where privacy could reliably be found. At one time, according to Aidan, it had been the only great hall at Highgate End.

"The council—"

"Nay." Aidan sat on the bench next to her. Despite its name, Wern Hall resembled a large chamber more than it did an actual hall. Only three trestle tables and a small high table adorned the small space. "In fact, I believe some progress was made today. With luck, an accord will be reached soon."

And Reid would be forced to go home.

"I will not let him leave without me."

"Then you should abandon your insistence that he and Gillian come to any sort of agreement. She will not yield." Aidan pointed to the oil lanterns on the wall. "Did you light those?"

"Aye," she said, pointing to a nearby candle. "I am not completely incapable."

"I never said such a thing."

Nay, but her sister had certainly made her feel that way. She'd retired early last eve, worn out from the emotional talk with Aidan as much as she was by the strain of avoiding Reid. This morn, she had intended to appeal to Gillian once again, but her sister had apparently gone to the village to supervise the gathering of supplies, a task they normally completed together. How was she to sway Gillian if Gillian would not even talk to her?

"You mentioned a war?" she asked as if inquiring about the weather.

Aidan smiled, apparently enjoying himself. "Gillian returned just as the council broke for the morning."

"You are maddening," Allie said with a shove. Aidan was being deliberately roundabout. "And?"

"And she had a few words to say about my advice to you—"

"So she overheard everything last eve."

Aidan shrugged. "So it would seem."

Allie sighed, defeated. If her sister was back, it was time for them to have a frank talk.

"She cannot understand why I am helping you. I was reciting all of Reid's, shall we say, finer qualities, when your betrothed—"

"We are not betrothed. Or not officially, of course."

"When your favorite Kerr brother overheard us."

Allie held her breath. "What did he do?"

Aidan's smile broadened. "Nothing. Which was when Graeme officially declared war."

"Graeme?"

"My stubborn brother came upon us and took Gillian's side, of course. I simply mentioned that Reid was doing nothing more than submitting himself to an unprovoked attack upon his character when—"

"Graeme told Aidan not to become involved," a newcomer to their conversation said from behind them.

Reid.

She and Aidan turned in tandem.

"You followed me here," Aidan said, though the accusation lacked heat.

"I did."

"Knowing I would tell Allie."

Reid walked toward them, but he didn't speak until he stood at Allie's side.

"And I thought your brother was the more intelligent of the two of you," he teased good-naturedly. "It seems I was mistaken."

Aidan clasped Reid's shoulder. "Though I admire your restraint back there, I must say, we may be on the losing side of this battle." He glanced at Allie. "Of course, the war has already been won. Your sister—"

"Will come to know Reid as I do," Allie said, her voice firm. "She'll have no choice."

Aidan looked back and forth between them, bowed, and then chuckled the entire way out of the hall.

Allie wanted to ask Reid why he hadn't come to her last night. Though she didn't dare admit it aloud, she'd waited for him until the wee hours of the night. In the morning, she'd felt totally unequal to the day ahead.

Her sister was angry. Her training, on hold. And Reid . . . perhaps he had thought better of being with someone whose family hated him. Even if he did deserve some of Gillian's ire.

All of those worries seemed to ebb away now that they were together. Nothing had been resolved, and yet it seemed to matter less now that they were together.

Reid sat atop the table opposite her, his feet on the bench below. "Good day, Lady Allie."

"Good day," she replied, though in truth it was not.

And then she remembered their last encounter. The tub. His fingers . . .

"You're embarrassed." Though he might not intend for it to

provoke, that lazy smile put her in mind of the day they'd met and his arrogant attempt to take her to bed.

"And you are enjoying it."

He continued to smile at her. "I am enjoying . . . the view."

Allie's pulse raced as it did every time he was near, which only made her more cross. "Reid, please be serious."

He was unapologetic. "I am."

"This is not a jest. Aidan said the meeting went well. When an accord is reached, you will leave. And if Gillian—"

He stood and reached for her before she could finish her thought.

"If your sister and her husband do not come around to our way of thinking, I will take you back to Brockburg with me, and you can convince them later."

He pulled her to her feet.

"I am not leaving here without you. We'll have our whole lives to make things right."

Reid brought his head down, claiming her lips, her mouth, her soul. She kissed him back with all of the longing she'd felt the night before and still felt now. He pulled back, just a bit, and took her lower lip between his teeth. He then kissed that same spot, slowly and gently, tugging and teasing. When Reid lifted her up against him, she grabbed him around his neck. He carried her to the edge of the table, sat her down, and gave her mouth the same attention he'd given it before moving her.

But this time he stood between her legs, his hands pushing them open until their bodies were pressed together.

Closer. She needed to be closer.

"Are we agreed?" he asked.

When he pulled away, it took Allie a moment to recover.

He wanted her to disobey the one person who'd always loved her. But she'd realized something in the whole Covington mess. While she still needed Gillian's love—and, indeed, always would—

she no longer needed her cosseting. She was no longer a child. Allie could decide what she wanted, and she wanted Reid.

"Aye," she said, feeling his breath against her face. Their eyes locked, an agreement passing between them.

"I will not leave here without you," he repeated.

Reluctantly, she responded, "Neither will I let you go."

It was not the way she wanted it to go, but as Aidan had said, they were at war. She, Reid, and Aidan on one side, Gillian and Graeme on the other. The outcome would not be as dramatic as that of the war being waged inside the solar of Highgate Castle, the one that would determine the course of the border clans' future. But it was her private battle, and to her it meant everything.

She intended to win.

Reid reached up and stroked her cheek with the back of his hand. That touch, so tender, strengthened her resolve. Gillian may think she knew all there was to know about Reid, but she was wrong. There was a softness in him that he did not allow others to see. Both sides did exist in the same man, but his loving nature was stronger than the front he put on for the world.

"Why do you push people away? There is such goodness in you—"

"And darkness too."

"So you say. But the goodness is stronger. It slips through even when you don't mean for it to happen." She threaded her fingers through his and laid them atop her lap. He still stood between her legs, the position more intimate in some ways than the day before in her bathtub.

"Just like there is a passion in you that demands to be set free."

Her expression had given her away. She couldn't stop thinking about that moment, his hands on her, inside her. Would it always be like that if they married?

"I never . . . I never knew."

"And now you do." He leaned toward her and kissed her,

slowly at first. She reveled in the softness of his lips, the slow, sensual movement as his mouth glided across hers, his tongue demanding attention. When the kiss became more insistent, she met his demands with some of her own.

Releasing his hand, Allie reached up and wrapped her arms around his neck, pulling him closer. Reid's groan encouraged her, and as she gave herself freely to him, she tried to forget about her sister and all the stumbling blocks that still lay between her and Reid. She allowed her fingers to stroke the side of his neck—

"Ahem."

Reid pulled back as they turned toward the interruption.

"Aidan?" She pushed Reid away, embarrassed to have been caught in such a position.

"I'm unconvinced such behavior will convince either Gillian or my brother to your cause."

Heat rushed up from Allie's neck to her cheeks. He was right, of course, but it seemed every time Reid was near, she was compelled to touch him, feel him next to her. She chanced a glance at Reid, who looked anything but embarrassed.

In fact, he was . . .

"You're gloating," she accused.

Allie looked from Reid to Aidan, whose amusement was on full display.

"And you," she spoke to Aidan. "Would not make a very good chaperone."

Her brother-in-law's laugh forced a smile from her despite their situation.

"Aye, you might be right about that. But you may want to come with me," he said to her. "You're wanted in the hall, and I did not think you would appreciate anyone but me finding you here."

"Gillian," Allie concluded.

"Nay," Aidan said. He nodded to Reid. "You're the one who's wanted."

Allie groaned. "Another lecture from your brother? I will come and speak to—"

"It's not Graeme who seeks you."

She looked from Aidan to Reid. Some silent message had passed between them, but Allie had no idea what it meant.

"Reid?"

But it was Aidan who spoke first.

"Your brother Alex is here."

15

"What are you doing here?" Reid asked.

"Is that any way to greet your brother?"

By the time Reid found Alex, the afternoon meetings had already begun. He had to sit through another brutal round of negotiation before he was able to speak to his brother alone.

As soon as a break was called, he and Alex walked away from the solar, away from the other men. Reid led his brother to a small alcove on the ground floor.

"Fancy you knowing all the hiding places," Alex said with a small smile as they sat on the stone bench perched inside of the nook. The words had been intended to tease, but he did not need a reminder of his tarnished reputation just now.

"I'm surprised to see you here."

Alex leaned back against the wall and folded his arms. "Some said talks were breaking down, that an accord would not be reached."

He and Alex shared such a likeness, people had oft thought them twins when they were younger. The key difference was the coloring of their hair—Reid's was much lighter. In some ways it had felt like they were twins, only Alex had always been in charge.

Despite his tepid greeting, Reid was pleased to see his brother. He'd missed him, though it wouldn't feel manly to say so. "Aye, indeed. And you thought to come here to help them?"

How very . . . Alex of him.

Alex shrugged. "I served as Toren's second for so long . . ."

"Move back," Reid said, his words sincere. "If you miss your position at Brockburg, come back and serve him again that way."

"Nay, that is not my intention." He leveled a serious look at Reid. "The position should be yours."

"Alex, do not—"

"Very well," Alex said quickly. "I didn't come here to continue that old argument."

They both went quiet as a servant entered the nook, bowed to both of them, and lit the wall torches. Neither of them spoke again until the man continued down the passageway.

"Then why did you come?" Reid pressed.

"I told you, I'd heard there was discord."

"As you saw this afternoon, you were right, but it appears as if an agreement is close. The only issue that remains is how precisely to deal with Caxton."

Though the chiefs continued to quibble, they'd begun to form a plan that would please all involved. The chiefs who'd jawed about boycotting the next Day of Truce had pledged to hold off so long as Douglas gave his word to ask King Alexander to consider new laws that would address the rampant blackmail on both sides of the border, ensuring harsher punishments for those found guilty. Only if the king and his English counterpart refused to come to new terms would the border clans attempt to find justice outside of March Law.

Alex shook his head. "With Caxton as Lord Warden, new laws will not matter. He is the worst of all offenders—"

"And the reason," Reid agreed, "that we are here." Some members of the council had actually argued for Caxton's murder. Others, like Douglas, believed more peaceable measures could be taken. "I fear we will never have peace with him in power."

"Agreed," his brother said. "What do we do about it?"

"A topic for another day," Reid said.

It struck him that Alex hadn't given him a straight answer about why he'd come. He was far from the only Scotsman who doubted Caxton's integrity, and with him in power, peace may very well crumble. But what did Alex hope to achieve by being here?

"How is my new niece?" he asked.

Alex and Clara's first baby had been born in May, four months earlier.

His brother's smile was so pure that Reid could not help but offer one of his own in return. Both of his brothers had been blessed with wonderful wives. Which reminded him of Allie, a topic he was not anxious to discuss. He'd have to explain himself soon enough.

"She and Clara are both doing well."

"I'm surprised you left them."

Though he'd not meant it as an insult, he could tell Alex took it as one.

"The outcome here will affect us all."

Reid stood and reached out his hand. "It will," he agreed, pulling his brother up off the bench.

"I suppose you are staying with me?" Although Highgate was a large castle with many rooms, it was filled to capacity for this council.

"Looking forward to it, brother."

"I hope you brought a bedroll."

"I am older."

"I am a better swordsman."

"A fact I shall allow you to prove tomorrow. In the meantime, I suppose a bedroll will do." Alex clasped him on the back. "The floor for you then. 'Tis good to see you."

"And you," he said, not looking forward to the reckoning there would be once the lord and lady of Highgate spoke to Alex about Allie.

But he was ready for it. For Allie, he would go through hell and back.

"WHAT THE HELL is wrong with you, Reid?"

Alex ignored the stares of those around them. They'd just finished a course of spiced fowl, and servants scurried throughout the hall carrying jugs of wine and ale. Highgate's cellarer and larderer spoke to the steward not far from them while the men at their table ate and drank in celebration. All knew, or at least hoped, their time at Highgate was nearing an end, and though the road ahead was fraught with dangers, for the first time since they'd arrived, a feeling of hopefulness prevailed.

Graeme had unfortunately spoken to Alex earlier, and while he'd not mentioned Allie, his brother had sensed something was wrong.

So Reid had told him everything.

"Wrong?" he asked. "Were you not listening, brother? I've done nothing to Lady Gillian." He lowered his voice. "Certainly not enough to warrant her continued ire."

Alex folded his arms.

Reid hated that look. He'd been receiving it since he was a child from both Alex and Toren.

"Perhaps I should not have agreed to train Allie," he did admit.

When Alex cleared his throat, Alex picked up his mug and finished the ale inside. Raising his mug for more, he waited until it was filled, and drank again.

Still, Alex said nothing.

"And I may have waited to show Allie such carnal pleasures as—"

"Reid, these are our hosts."

His brother's tone set Reid on edge. He drank again, and this time, he did not attempt to make excuses.

When the man next to Alex leaned over and raised his mug for a toast, Alex complied. Their discussion ceased, thankfully, until the meal was over. Alex nodded toward the hall's entrance. And with a final glance at Allie, whom he'd indulged himself in looking at throughout the meal despite Alex's repeated warnings, he followed his brother out.

"Not here."

This was precisely why he'd not mentioned it earlier.

As they descended the stairs to the ground floor, Alex's expression turned increasingly grim. The moment they were outside the castle doors, his brother turned on him. "You taunt our hosts, threaten our alliance with de Sowlis, and smile about both," he said.

Darkness had descended, and the courtyard was mostly empty.

"I did nothing, brother, you and Toren did not do before me. I care for her."

I love her.

He started to walk away from the keep, but Alex followed him. "You've been warned away in no uncertain terms."

"And if you had been warned away from Clara? By anyone other than the lady herself? You would have done what? Given up?" He did not back down despite the tick in his brother's jaw.

"I would not have tossed decorum in the face of my hosts. And if you'd heeded such tenets of common courtesy, Lady Gillian would not have such strong feeling against you."

"I apologize," he said. His tone was becoming belligerent, but he found he didn't much care. "If only I were as perfect as you, Lady Gillian would have fallen at my feet."

"Reid, this is not about me."

"No, this is about us. Would it have been so difficult for you to be happy for me? Glad that I found someone who makes me better than I am?"

"I am happy for you," Alex said, pulling him to a stop. "But you have to be smarter about how—"

"Like you. What you mean to say is that I should be more like you." He loved his brother, hated fighting with him. But he said the words anyway.

"Calm down, Reid."

Words assured to make him anything but calm.

"Why are you here, Alex?" he snapped. "Tell me the real reason." His hands shook at his sides as rage built up within him.

Alex ground his teeth together, his jaw tightening. Reid had managed to shake his brother's composure. Good.

"Say it, Alex. Say it," he taunted.

"Reid—"

"You are here because you don't trust me."

"That is not true."

"Or at least because you think you represent Clan Kerr better than I do."

Alex clenched his own fists. Sometimes Reid wished his brother would strike out and hit him. In a strange way, he thought it would make him feel better. At least he'd know he wasn't the only Kerr totally incapable of self-control.

"You go too far, brother."

No, he hadn't. Not yet.

"Go home, Alex. Go back to Dunmure Tower."

Some of the fight went out of Alex, replaced with a very different emotion. He'd hurt his brother.

Good.

"Words spew from your mouth," Alex ground out, "and you don't care who you hurt with them."

And his brother had said *he* was the one whose words sliced? "You are right," he said, lowering his voice. "I don't care."

With that, he pushed past his brother and strode back toward the castle.

Allie and her sister stood just outside the door. They looked at him in mute shock, their eyes wide. So they'd heard it all.

"Allie—"

"No," she said. "Not now."

Gillian looked every bit as cold and judgmental as she always did when he was around.

He had to get out of there.

Rather than go inside, Reid turned back around, ignoring his brother, and walked away from Alex. Away from Gillian.

Away from Highgate End and the only woman who had ever looked at him with the kind of respect Allie did.

Until now.

16

"Don't say it."

After Reid and his brother left, Allie wanted to fall into the well in the center of the courtyard. Facing her sister after what they'd heard . . . it was nearly as difficult as watching Reid walk away without stopping him.

"I said nary a word."

A servant opened the great wooden doors, and sounds from the revelry upstairs filtered down to them.

"You should get back—"

"Talk to me, Allie."

You are right. I don't care. Reid's words still echoed in her ears.

"He was angry—"

"Nay, Allie. That's who he is. Of all the men in Scotland, or England, you would choose one who acts that way?"

Allie didn't know what to think. Deep inside, she knew Reid had spoken to Alex that way out of anger. And yet . . .

"You brought me here to speak to him." Gillian took both of her hands. "And I came. But you will not convince me that my sister . . . my wonderful, adventurous, sweet sister . . . should wed a man who speaks in such a way to someone he loves."

Her shoulders tingled with the compliment despite the words that came after it.

"You are in pain," Gillian said, reaching out to touch her cheek. "I see it. I see the way you look at him."

She attempted a smile. "I thought I'd hidden it well."

Gillian's sad smile made her feel even worse. "You forget, I've been sitting at meals with you for over twenty years."

"Even when I was a baby?" she jested.

Gillian wrapped her arms around her. "Aye, even as a baby," she whispered in her ear. "Mother and I would argue about it, in fact. I could not bear to put you down. Ever."

She pulled back and looked into her sister's eyes.

"I have a confession," Gillian said.

Her very proper sister, a confession?

"I knew—" Gillian took her by the hand and led her away from the keep. They walked the length of the courtyard. "—about your training."

Allie froze. "You—"

"I knew you left the keep before sunset most days, after the men had vacated the outer training yard. So I followed you one day. What I still don't understand is why. And why did you keep it from me?"

She wasn't sure she could explain, so she ignored the questions and asked one of her own. "When you found me with Reid . . . you seemed surprised."

"To find you with him, aye."

They walked up the same stairs Allie had been ascending *that* night, the one Reid had called her down. The night they'd pledged themselves to each other. The memory was almost too much to bear.

"I could not believe my sister had fallen in love with such a man," she said as they reached the wall-walk.

Gillian said it so quietly, it took a moment for her words to pierce the thick fog that seemed to surround Allie's brain. It was true, of course. Though Allie had never been in love before, Reid consumed her every thought. When she was with him, her body screamed and her mind muddled with the desire to feel him next to her. She wanted to know everything about him, be with him always.

"How did you know?"

They peered out into the darkness. Moonlight and light from a few nearby torches allowed them to see into the outer courtyard but not much beyond it.

"As I said, Allie. I know you perhaps as well as you know yourself. Which is why I am so surprised you're attracted to such a man."

"Gill, please understand—"

"I'm sorry. I cannot."

When she looked at her sister, Allie's chest felt as if someone were trampling it. "Please—"

"I will always, always do what is best for you. And I do not believe Reid Kerr is that." Gillian paused, then added, "I would ask something of you."

Allie already knew she would not like this.

Gillian heaved a sigh. "I know you will not heed my advice if I ask for you to forget him. All I am asking is that you do not do anything rash."

"But I—"

"Please. Just do not give yourself to him, or marry him . . . a man you hardly know. Allow some time to pass first. Be sure of your feelings."

Hope soared through her.

"And if I do give it time? You will accept him?"

"I cannot wish for you to share your life with such a man. I ask you to do this only because if you wait, I believe you will see what I do. That there are other men, like Graeme and Aidan—"

Allie hated being angry at her sister, but the bargain hardly seemed fair. "You ask me to do this for you, yet you offer nothing in return. What about my happiness? Could I not ask you to accept him for my sake?"

Gillian sighed. "I want you to be happy . . . *that* is why I would ask you to wait."

Her sister truly believed Reid was not right for her. She wanted to rail at Gillian, but her sister was obviously acting out of love.

If she agreed to wait, it would devastate Reid. They'd promised to stay together . . . but she could admit there might be some merit to Gillian's plan. It was true she hardly knew him . . .

Her intuition told her he was the one for her, the only one, but she'd only had the freedom to make her own decisions for such a short while.

"Very well," she said reluctantly. "I will not do anything 'rash,' as you say. But by St. Crispin's Day, if nothing has changed—"

"I will take you to Brockburg myself."

Though you will still hate Reid.

She did not voice the thought aloud. Allie did not need confirmation of what she already knew.

"I am doing this for you. But understand, Gillian, nothing will change. You said I love Reid, and you were right. I do." Nothing would change her mind about him, not even the kind of deplorable behavior that had set Gillian's mind against him earlier. If only her sister would trust her to know her own mind, or trust that Reid must have merit if she had fallen in love with him.

As to that. She should probably wait to speak to Reid until tomorrow, but Allie had never been a particularly patient person.

Reid pounded his fist on the table, making the jug of ale rattle. Noticing it, he poured ale into his mug until it nearly spilled over. He'd been hesitant to return to his bedchamber, but it would seem Alex had found other accommodations for the evening.

Unsurprising after what he'd said to his brother.

Reid drained the ale much too quickly and poured himself another. After the scene with Alex, he'd gone into the hall and liberated a jug from one of the serving maids. Another infraction against him, no doubt.

Dammit, Reid.

He'd gone from cursing his brother to shifting the blame precisely where it belonged. What was wrong with him? Alex had asked him the same thing, but he couldn't give an answer. Why did he insist on provoking everyone, including the people he loved?

Reid considering leaving to find Alex, but something held him back. Toren would say it was the streak of Kerr stubbornness that all three of them possessed. But it was more than that. Reid had nothing to say.

Alex had been right. About everything.

He'd been careless . . . and foolish . . . knowing Gillian despised him, Reid should have taken more care.

He truly didn't deserve Allie.

A soft knock at the door wrested him out of his thoughts. Reid opened it and froze.

"You shouldn't be here." He did not move or invite Allie inside. He did, however, glance down at her boys' breeches and shirt.

"I must speak with you."

Reid motioned inside. "In here? Do you believe that is a—"

She wasn't asking. Allie pushed her way around him and entered on her own accord.

He gripped the side of the door so hard his knuckles turned white. She should not be in here. Reid was not strong enough to leave her completely untouched. Even now, when he turned back toward her, his instinct was to toss her on his bed and ensure no one could question his right to marry her.

"How could you say such a thing?" she asked.

She was hurt, of course. He had sounded cold even to his own ears. Lashing out had been his specialty for so long—it was nigh on impossible to stop.

Reid closed his eyes and groaned. Having never practiced, he had not realized how difficult it would be to say the words aloud. When he opened his eyes, she stood there, calm . . . still . . . waiting. She looked curious rather than angry, as if she genuinely did not understand him.

"I did not mean it," he started.

Nay, I can't do this.

Allie moved toward him, but he held out an arm to stop her. He did not deserve to be comforted.

"No," she said. "You will not." She swatted at his arm, refusing to back down. "Tell me how you could be so hurtful, so uncaring to your own brother?"

When she looked at him that way, Reid wanted to fall onto his knees, wrap his arms around her and beg forgiveness. She was so good. So loving. The glib remark he'd planned stuck in his throat.

"I . . ." He shrugged.

"You don't know."

Allie took another step toward him and cupped his face as she'd done once before.

"I will not allow you to push me away like that. You can say you don't care how your actions affect others, but I know otherwise. So shall we try this again?"

Her hands felt like two angel's wings embracing him, holding him rooted to the spot. He couldn't have turned away had he wanted to. She peered into his eyes, almost daring him to try.

"I'm sorry."

"I know you are."

"Your sister—"

"Is angrier than ever. But we've plenty of time to speak about that. I want to know . . . why Reid? Why do you say things you do not mean?"

Because it's easier that way. Because it's what's expected of me.

When he didn't answer, Allie moved her hands from his face to his waist. He wrapped his arms around her shoulders and closed his eyes as she lay her head on his chest. He listened to her even breathing, not speaking or even making a move to explore her soft curves with his hands. They stood there that way for so long, Reid began to wonder if she had fallen asleep.

"Do not ever attempt that with me," she demanded.

"I will not," he promised.

"And you will apologize to your brother—"

"I'd already planned on it. And your sister too."

Allie picked her head up and looked at him. "Nay, not her."

"But—"

"I was wrong, Reid. A few days will not change her opinion. And now, after that performance . . ."

"What?" He didn't like the look in her eyes. Could she be having second thoughts?

"I may have told her . . ."

When she tried to pull away, Reid held on to her. "What did you tell her?"

"I told her . . . I told her I would not do anything rash."

"Such as?"

"Take you to my bed."

When they both looked at his bed, she added, "Or allow you to take me to yours."

He pulled back and shrugged. "'Tis not so bad. I—"

"That is not all."

He really, really did not care for Allie's sister.

"I promised to give it time. For us not to—"

He stepped back. "No. We made a promise. I will not leave here without you."

The very thought filled him with panic. If he left her here with her sister, there was a chance, no matter how small, her sister would succeed in persuading her.

"You will. Just until St. Crispin's Day—"

"Is this some sort of cruel jest? Did you really agree to that?"

Allie looked tired suddenly. He wanted to pick her up in his arms, carry her to the bed, and show her exactly what he thought of Lady Gillian's decree.

"Suffice it to say Gillian does not believe you are the best man for me," she said. And though regret dripped from every word, it pained him to hear it said aloud.

"She believes I need time away from you"—Allie smiled, but he could not even pretend to do the same—"and the undeniable pull you have on me."

"No."

She would not be deterred. "My sister loves me and has been protecting me her entire life. She asked, and I agreed to make her happy. For her, I would agree to almost anything."

"Allie, this is madness."

"This changes nothing," she said. "I want to be with you, Reid. We *will* be together. But if I can make Gillian feel better about the match, I will."

He didn't like it and was prepared to tell her so when Alex's words came back to him.

I am happy for you.

Instead of believing him, Reid had fought back. Why couldn't he trust the people he loved? Believe them?

"Can we not enjoy the remaining time you have here?" she pressed, then looked down. "And Gillian isn't all wrong. We've only just met. Maybe we should both take a little time to ensure this is what we want."

He cupped her face gently, angling it up so their eyes met.

"It matters not. If we'd met just this eve I would already know. I love you, Allie. I've never said that to a woman before, and I'll never say it to another one. I love you and want you to be my wife."

She placed her hands over his. "And I love you, Reid."

Every muscle in his body relaxed at the sound of those three beautiful words. He placed a kiss on her lips so tender that even as his body willed him to take more, he wanted only to stand there, in her presence, allowing the goodness that was Lady Allie Bowman to overwhelm all of him, to wash over him and make him somehow better.

He did not need any more than that. For now.

17

"Your feet must change positions more quickly."

Allie tried to concentrate, but Reid's intense gaze made her lose focus. He was still very much a mystery in some ways. At times, he appeared so serious that Allie was sure he contemplated a purpose so deep it would take years to uncover it. But he also tended to be the center of joviality. Whenever she heard laughter at the midday meal, she would dart a glance at Reid's table, and more often than not, she'd see the men around him laughing uproariously and clapping him on the back. Even so, some of the men regarded him with a leery look, as if they feared he'd use his way with words against them.

He stood back and lifted his own sword in front of him at shoulder height. "Front foot back. Move your sword, turning with the hilt and changing your feet at the same time."

As he moved, the muscles beneath his tunic strained.

"My feet," he said, cutting back and forth. "You're looking at my feet."

But she clearly was not.

Reid stopped what he was doing, waiting for her to shift her attention. When she did, he resumed the cutting drill, but it was still quite impossible for her to focus on his technique. He stopped abruptly, his eyes narrowing at her.

"I thought you wanted to learn," he teased, moving toward her.

Allie raised her sword. "I do."

He met her sword with his own. "You think to stop my advance?"

Truth be told, she didn't want to.

"Aye," she said, full of false bravado.

He tapped and thrusted, testing her. Allie pulled from every one of her sword-fighting lessons and met each of his movements as skillfully as she was able. She tried to forget about his high cheekbones and his muscular body and remember to move her feet as quickly as her sword.

Then he smiled, a slow, sensual smile that robbed Allie of her next breath and saw her sword knocked to the ground. He was next to her immediately, grabbing her wrist with his free hand.

"You forgot our first lesson," he said. Allie licked her bottom lip in anticipation.

She struggled to remember what he spoke of. All she could think of was kissing him.

"And now you will suffer for it." His eyes told her a very different story. They held a wicked promise.

"It sounds dreadful."

His face was close enough to hers that she could feel his breath on her cheek. Lowering his head toward hers, Reid took her lower lip in his mouth. In the next moment, he took everything. Covering her lips with his own, he thrust his tongue inside without apology. The kiss was demanding, but Allie did not mind. In fact, the more he demanded, the more she gladly gave. A warmth enveloped her as she returned the kiss with vigor.

Reid pulled back, his eyes hooded. "If this continues, the promise you made to your sister will not stand."

"Why?" she asked, feigning innocence.

Though he was in complete control, restraint overcoming the desire she knew he felt, Allie was sure she could break through.

Now why would you do that?

"Because," he drawled. "Every time I touch you, every time my lips taste you, I want more. Do you remember, sweet Allie, that feeling in the tub?"

As if she could ever forget.

She nodded. "Aye, very well."

"I will make it my life's purpose to give you that same pleasure every day we're together."

"But what—"

"Though, I am no monk," he continued. "There will come a time when you will do the same to me. I can wait."

She inadvertently looked down. Did he mean—

He turned away then, his shoulders rising and falling.

"Reid?"

He tilted his head back and squeezed his eyes shut, groaning loudly in frustration, before he turned to face her once again.

"Training," he said. "We should get back to the training."

Allie smiled. "Are you saying you have difficulty restraining yourself when you're this close to me?" Of course, she knew the answer. Reveled in it.

"Aye, lass. Very much so."

"Hmmm," she said, taking a step toward him. "Then would you mind if I—"

He jumped back from her touch so quickly that Allie forgot her game for a moment. "How do you move so quickly?"

Reid tossed his training sword next to hers on the ground.

"You mean, like this?" He took off running toward the dovecote.

Allie followed, but when she arrived at the old building, he was nowhere to be seen. She looked inside and around the back, but—

"Ahhh!" she shrieked when a hand caught her waist from behind.

A moment later, when Reid pressed her back up against the stone building, her heart quickened for an entirely different reason.

"Reid, you scared me," she said.

"And you, my dear Allie, do the same with me."

She reached up to tuck an errant strand of his hair back in place. His side was pressed up against her, but he did not attempt to come any closer.

"Tell me," she coaxed, the playfulness of the previous moment forgotten. "Why do you show me and no one else?"

He knew exactly what she meant—she could see it in his expression.

"A good question, lass."

She blinked, waiting. He wasn't going to answer.

"Tell me something," she said, "something I do not know."

As Reid contemplated her words, Allie contented herself by listening to the soft sound of rustling leaves in the distance. Some small animal, perhaps? Otherwise, she could hear only Reid's breathing.

"Do you know anything of my family?"

"Very little," she said honestly. "I know you have a sister and two brothers, and that Toren is chief."

"And became so after my father died in battle. I was the only one of my brothers who was not there with him that day, as I was just ten and three. Toren and Alex . . ."

"Are older," she finished.

"They could have taken me with them," he said, "but they did not."

He wasn't looking at her any longer. After a moment of silence, she asked, "And your mother? Graeme said she came back into your lives."

Reid's eyes met hers again. "Aye, two summers ago. She left after my father was killed. Abandoned us, or so we believed. Alex would never let it go. Every so often, he would ride out to England to look for her."

That surprised her. "Your mother is English?"

"It seems my father began a family tradition," he said. "Aye, she is English."

She had so many questions. How could a mother have abandoned her children at such a time? And how could they have forgiven her for it?

"You see, she was betrothed to a cruel man before she married my father. After she was widowed, this man came to Scotland and threatened her. He told her he would kill all of her children if she did not return with him."

"Kill you?"

"She believed him," he said, seeming to understand her incredulity. "He'd snuck into Brockburg, and he told her that same stealth could be used against us. No matter how long it took, he would kill each and every one of her children. And so . . . she left."

Although he tried to mask his pain, Allie could see what his mother's leaving, no matter what her reasons, had done to him. How it affected him still.

"How was she able to return? Did your brother—"

"Kill him? Nay, that is our only regret. By the time Alex found our mother, her new husband had died and she was living with his tyrannical son."

"So your brother brought her back to Scotland?"

"He did. Our mother was eager to see us, but she was terrified we would hate her after what she'd done." Reid closed his eyes.

"But Alex found her. And you have a mother once again."

"Aye," he said with a sigh that told her his story had come to an end. "And your parents? What of them?"

"Hmm," she said. "My tale is not so long as that. My father cares for Lyndwood and his position as an important border lord more than he does his family. My mother obeys him in all things.

They love us, but not in the way I would hope to love my own children."

"*Our* children?"

Allie felts a rush of pleasure at his words.

Reid stood back and smiled. "I do believe we shall be sure to do it better. Our wee ones will never question our love for them."

There was a teasing glint in his eyes, and he leaned toward her in a way that reminded her of their earlier chase, only he clearly intended to be the predator this time.

Well, she would show him. She was determined to outrun him. She only waited for the right moment.

"And I do believe we should start . . . right now," he said, his grin spreading wider.

Allie turned and ran as fast as her legs would go, laughing and pushing past branches, knowing he would catch up with her soon.

18

"And now, we celebrate."

Twenty-two men cheered, as jovial a scene as could be achieved with such a group, but Reid's world seemed to close in around him. After less than a fortnight, his time at Highgate had come to an end.

In the end, Alex's connections had made a difference. He and the Lord Warden had always shared a special bond, and it was Alex who'd finally convinced the Lord Warden to do as all the border chieftains insisted and reject the selection of Caxton as the English warden.

Douglas had agreed that neither he nor the Scottish wardens under him would meet with him. They would not treat with a man who was known to accept bribes that put the Scots in danger. Douglas had pledged to inform the king of the border lords' decision. If it led to a breakdown of the truce—so be it. It was the decision of the men who ruled from east to west.

It was a compromise, of sorts, allaying those who were ready for battle now and pacifying others who thought continued negotiation was the only way to peace.

"Well done, brother."

Alex frowned. "It is far from over."

Reid silently agreed.

"If negotiations fall apart, and even if they do not," his brother said, his eyes troubled. "Our clan, our brother . . . they will need the guidance that you can offer them."

God, how he hated this particular subject. "I've told you, and him—"

"I understand what you've said, and I understand more than you realize about your reluctance to take the position, but you truly are the best man—"

"Not now, brother—"

"It should be you. Reid, you are a better man than all of us. If only you—"

He could not have this discussion now. Instead, he stood and made a comment about Toren's strength and another to adequately dismiss himself from his brother.

Reid made his way down to the ground floor of the keep, walked out into the courtyard and did not stop. He strode through the gatehouse and, without registering where he was going, found himself in the one place he'd found solace during his time at Highgate End.

Of course, the woods were dark and empty. He wandered the makeshift training yard until he found the spot where he'd first suggested taking over Allie's training. He'd realized that afternoon she was not only adept with the longsword, she was quite good. There were men who'd trained for much, much longer without becoming so skilled. He was proud of her.

As he was of Alex.

And yet he was, by his own design, alone. He'd rejected Alex as he had Toren and his clan. Of course he supported his brother, and would continue to do so. But just not in the way they wanted.

Reid picked up a small rock and tossed it into the air as hard as he could throw it. A distant splash surprised him.

Pushing his way through the branches, he came upon a stream

running from north to south. As he discarded his boots and moved toward it, Reid could see it was plenty deep enough for a bath.

———

THE MOMENT it became clear Reid would not be attending the dinner, Allie had attempted to leave in search of him. But Gillian had tugged her back into her seat.

"If you go to him," she said, "you will not keep your vow." It was the first Gillian had spoken of the matter in days. Surely she knew Allie and Reid had continued to train together. She must also have seen the stolen glances at meals.

Though she clearly did not like it, Gillian had said nothing.

Until tonight.

"Of course I will," Allie insisted. "I made a promise."

"I see the way you look at him, and he at you. Unless you plan to follow my path—"

"Which I would be glad to do," she said, referring to her sister's marriage.

Gillian frowned. "'Tis rumored Reid and his brother fought after the council's decision this morn."

"No rumor," Graeme added. Although he'd been looking out at the crowd, he had apparently heard every word. "I have remained silent on the matter until now—"

Allie was most curious for his opinion.

"—but I have known Reid Kerr my whole life as an ally of Clan Scott."

"As have I," Aidan said from his seat beside her. But she continued to watch Graeme.

"And I agree with everyone. He is loyal and protective and would undoubtedly keep you safe."

Allie smiled.

"But he is also arrogant and lost. He is spurning a position that should be his and weakening his clan because of it."

Her eyes searched the hall once more. Nothing. His brother was nowhere to be found either. And if she did find him, would Allie comfort him or knock some sense into the man she would take as a husband?

Likely both.

"Alex—"

"Returned to Dunmure Tower after the council's decision."

For one awful moment, Allie wondered if Reid could have left without at least bidding her goodbye.

"He is still here," Graeme said, though Allie could not be sure how he knew her thoughts.

"I would also urge caution," he said, nodding to Gillian. "With some time apart, and perhaps a visit to Brockburg—"

"Graeme!" Gillian did not appear pleased with the idea of going to Reid's home.

But her husband was not deterred. "We hardly knew each other when we married, and our outcome was a happy one."

The rest of the meal passed in a blur, and although Aidan compelled her to dance, she did not once forget this was Reid's last night at Highgate. As soon as she could leave without causing a fuss, she did so. Only after she'd left the hall did she realize she wasn't sure where to go.

Should she seek him out in his chamber?

Nay.

Surely he had his reasons for not seeking her out on his last night at the keep. She would not go looking for him. But neither was she ready to retire.

In the end, Allie wandered the ramparts, the cool night air making her wish she'd brought a cape. When she couldn't take the cold anymore, let alone the constant thoughts and worries about Reid—she circled around and headed to her bedchamber.

As she stepped through the door, it occurred to her that

Gillian hadn't had any cause to worry, but it was only because Reid had shown restraint, not her. Had it been up to her, they would have spent this last evening alone together. The thought made her laugh a little despite herself.

"Care to tell me what is so amusing?"

Sitting across from the entrance, his legs outstretched and arms folded as if he'd been waiting patiently for some time, was Reid.

"Good evening, Allie."

19

She wore white.

It was an unusual gown for an unusual woman. Sweet, innocent, pure. Adventurous, beautiful, untamed. Allie was all of those things, and more.

If she was surprised to see him there, she didn't show it. Instead, she closed the door behind her with a finality that prickled his skin.

"You're wet."

Of all the things he'd expected her to say, that was not one of them. Reid ran his hand through his hair, confirming that it was indeed still damp from his frigid dip in the stream.

"You're mine."

Like so many of his words of late, they came out wrong. He hadn't meant them to sound harsh, demanding. He'd only meant that, although he was leaving on the morrow, he would not go a moment without thinking of her. Wanting her. Loving her.

He jumped to his feet, intending to take what he'd said back, but instead he found himself stalking toward her. In truth, she made it easy, standing beside the door in that white gown, her hair piled atop her head like she was some ancient virgin sacrifice.

He longed to touch her—to never stop touching her—but when his hand reached out, it was only to remove one of the pins that held up her hair. She watched him as carefully as she always did in training, as if attempting to anticipate his next move. He'd taught her what to expect out there. But here, in this room, when they were alone . . . she still had much to learn.

"You never came to dinner."

After the fight with his brother, he had not been inclined to speak with anyone but the one person he cared most to be near. And he also had not trusted himself to be in the presence of others on their final night together. With good cause. But he was here now, and he would ensure she did not forget him until they were together again.

He removed another pin, and then another. When the last pin's tenuous hold gave way, he watched as her hair tumbled down around her.

"When you wake tomorrow," he said, tossing the pins to the ground, "you will feel the lingering touch of my lips on yours." He raised his finger and gently swept it over her lower lip. He moved closer. "The press of my body on yours will feel so real that closing your eyes will bring it all back with achingly sweet clarity."

Her lips parted and it took all of Reid's restraint not to accept the invitation. She was still so innocent, but desire flickered in her eyes. Part of him wanted to inflame that desire until they were both consumed. But the other, the part of him Allie saw so clearly, was the one that would claim victory this eve.

Though he would still make good on his promise to ensure she awoke with very real memories of this night.

"Close your eyes."

That Allie did so immediately endeared her to him even more.

He took the slightest step back so that only the very tips of her breasts touched his chest. As much as he wanted to pull her into his arms, Reid did not. He waited until she became impatient and opened her eyes.

"Keep them closed, lass," he insisted.

As she shut them again, the air between them seemed to sizzle with anticipation. Every feature on her face was so perfectly formed that Reid almost reached up to touch her. But restraint won the day.

When she finally stopped moving, anticipating, Reid moved in. He slid his hands up between them, his palms facing her. He allowed them to hang in the air for a moment before he reached for the neckline of her gown.

What if she has a particular penchant for the garment and its shift underneath?

Reid decided to take a chance. And despite the heaviness of the gown, with one swift motion, he tore the material in two and pushed it open, revealing the prize beneath. Two perfectly formed creamy orbs tipped with dark nipples begging for his mouth.

Cupping both breasts at once, he used his thumb to ensure her nipples were hard and ready for him. Then he sucked and nipped at one of them until she groaned. When he looked up to ensure he'd not been too rough, his love's face was filled with wonderment and pleasure. He did it again, this time using his other hand to give the breast the attention it deserved.

By the time Reid stood up straight, his cock stood up with him, hard and begging for relief. He could see from Allie's expression he'd only accomplished part of his goal. She would remember him tomorrow, and every day they were apart, but she wanted more. Reid wanted her to think of nothing beyond the pleasure he'd given her. So when he saw an opening in her partially torn dress, he took it.

Reaching below her undergarments, Reid didn't stop until he felt the soft curls that stood guardian to her very core.

"Look at me."

She'd already been doing so, but he didn't want her to look away. Reid wanted her to know that pleasing her gave him as much enjoyment as it did her.

He needed her to know how she affected him.

Reid didn't glide his fingers in as slowly and smoothly as he'd done in the tub. This time, once ensuring she was wet and ready for him, he plunged inside, fitting his palm against her. He circled and thrusted, relentless, watching as her lips parted and her eyes opened wide.

When she was close, Reid backed them both up against the wall as her soft moans became louder, a flush creeping from her neck to her face.

"Oh yes," she panted. Still, he did not relent. When she finally cried out, he cupped her curls and waited patiently for her breathing to slow back down to normal. Only then did he pull away.

Her gown was torn in two, her hair completely tousled.

She looked down in something like shock. "'Tis torn."

He chuckled. "Aye, lass, very much so. Though I cannot apologize."

"Why?"

"I will never lie to you." He looked directly at her. "I am not sorry for wanting to be with you so much that the thought of removing that obstacle by any other means never entered my mind."

Allie reached down and pulled the torn pieces together.

"It was an old gown anyway," she said with a sly smile. "Though I will need another, or perhaps two, to replace it."

Reid took her hands in his. "Gowns, family, love . . . I will give it all to you, Allie. I wish to do so right now."

And in that moment, when she looked at him with such reverence, every argument he'd given his brothers fell away. She loved him. Believed in him. And since he valued her judgment, just maybe—

"Soon." She smiled. "In the meantime, I do believe you are correct . . ."

"About?"

"Tomorrow." She glanced down at where her hands held the gown in place. "This shall be quite difficult to forget."

"Well then," he said with a formal bow. "My job here is done."

"But you—"

"Must leave," he said. "If I stay here much longer, we will begin our lives together at a disadvantage, for I will have earned your sister's ire and broken a promise to my new brother-in-law."

At her confused expression, he clarified. "Another moment longer and that dress will lie in two at your feet and you will be my wife in all but formality."

2 0

———————

$\mathcal{W}$alking away from Allie's room last eve was the hardest thing he'd ever done, but now he'd have to leave her in truth.

"Lady Gillian, a word?"

He'd lingered for as long as possible. The border chiefs and their men had been riding away from Highgate all morning. Douglas had already left for Edinburgh and an audience with the king.

It was time for him to go too, to leave Highgate's hall and return to Brockburg.

"I don't believe we have anything to—"

"Please, my lady. Just one word."

He saw Allie out of the corner of his eye. The look she gave him promised that she was, indeed, thinking of their night together. But there was also a sadness to her that he felt himself as keenly as any blow he'd received in battle. He promised himself he would find a way to be alone with her for one last moment before leaving.

"Very well," she said, guiding him toward the circular stairwell that led to the ground floor. Her husband, Aidan, Allie . . . they all watched from the table on the dais.

"You do not like me," he started.

Gillian's frown looked so similar to Allie's that it took him aback for a moment.

"That is not so," she said. "I simply do not like you for my sister." She looked hesitant to continue. "Whether you're the man I first met at The Wild Boar or the one who Graeme, Aidan, and now Allie tell me is buried deep within, I do not know. But with my sister, I will not take unnecessary chances."

"My lady," he pleaded. "Allow me a chance to show you which man asks for your sister's hand in marriage." He took a deep breath, not ready for this. But after visiting Allie the evening before, he'd been thinking of nothing but her and the words he was about to utter. So he forged ahead. "The man you met thought little of himself. You see, he'd refused his chief's call to stand next to him." His gaze did not waver despite the irreversible words he would speak. "The one who stands before you now is worthy of that position. Is worthy to take his brother's place. Is worthy of your sister's love." He rushed the words out before she could stop him. "With your permission, I will return to Brockburg, ensure my clan enforces the terms agreed upon here, and take my rightful place in Clan Kerr. And then I will marry your sister."

Lady Gillian was as intimidating as any man he'd ever faced in any tournament or battle. In the end, he was determined to marry Allie, and neither Gillian or her husband would deter him, but he knew how much this woman's approval meant to her.

"I would ask you one question."

He knew that determined look, had seen it before. Mayhap the sisters had more in common than he'd thought. Reid fought a smile, knowing she would misunderstand.

"Why did you refuse your brother?"

Reid startled. She'd asked him the one question he could not easily answer.

"My lady." He shook his head. "I do not—"

"You ask for the most precious gift in the world," she said, more kindly than she'd spoken to him yet. "And despite my feelings for you, I find myself wavering."

He took a deep breath and glanced up at the lingering guests in the hall, Allie among them. A tightness gripped his chest and refused to let go.

He looked back at Gillian.

Dammit.

"I did not believe the elders would agree."

"And why would they not do so?"

Reid didn't think she would appreciate a litany of his bad behaviors, so instead he settled for another hard truth. One unlikely to bring Lady Gillian to his side. "I did not deserve it."

He could tell he'd managed to surprise her. Hell, he'd surprised himself. But the last thing he wanted to do was continue their conversation down such a path. "Now, if you'll excuse me, my lady, I would like to say goodbye to your sister."

After Gillian's slight nod, he caught Allie's eye. She came to him, and without another word, they walked away from all of the curious eyes and out into the courtyard.

It was too beautiful a day for this discussion.

A groom brought horse after horse out from the stables. It was yet another reminder that he was due to leave as well. Wanting a more private discussion, Reid led her to the side of the courtyard.

"If I could, I would tear that dress as I did last eve until you were gloriously naked in front of me." Reid lowered his voice, the knave in him impatient. "And I would cherish your body, little by little, until no bit of flesh was left unworshiped."

He leaned closer.

"And then I would guide myself into you, slowly, reverently, joining us for all eternity."

Two small pinks spots appeared on Allie's cheeks. "What makes you believe I'd allow such a thing?"

The sparkle of amusement in her eyes was the reason he resisted dragging her to a more secluded spot to test her words. "I do not doubt that you would," he said, not masking the confidence in his voice, "but he would not."

Allie turned toward Graeme and then looked back to him.

"Thank you," she said.

Reid raised a brow.

"For allowing me an opportunity to sway my sister."

"I will be back for you."

"I know."

He wanted to tell her about his plan to fight for his rightful place by his brother's side first, but the words would not come out.

"And we will be married."

"Aye," she agreed, the determination on her face making their parting only slightly less painful.

"Will you continue to train while I'm gone?"

"I will best you someday," she boasted, and Reid did not doubt it.

They were being watched, and as such, he could not kiss her. But he would not leave without at least one final contact. Taking her hand in his, he brought it to his lips and kissed the palm, lingering as long as he was able.

"Until we meet again," he said, stepping back, a chill overtaking him as he stepped away from her.

"I love you," she said, softly, sweetly.

"And I love you."

ALLIE WOULD NOT HAVE IMAGINED her day could get any worse. After Reid had left, she'd spent the better part of the afternoon assisting Gillian in offering farewells to the various chiefs. All her smiles had been faked.

How had a man she'd just met crept his way into her heart and claimed a piece of her she'd not known was available for someone to claim?

And now this. She'd seen the horses arrive with her own eyes but could hardly believe it.

"'Tis not possible," she said for the second time to Morgan.

And yet it was. When Allie walked into the great hall, she knew him immediately, no matter that he was facing away from her. She'd seen that stance before. Many, many times.

Allie put one foot in front of the other, forcing herself closer to what she knew would be, at best, an uncomfortable greeting. At worse, it signaled trouble for her. With each step, a heaviness settled into her chest until she was merely a few steps away from him.

Taking a deep breath, and ignoring Gillian's worried expression as she saw her approach, Allie greeted him.

"Father."

He turned toward her. "Allie."

She embraced him even though she knew it made him uncomfortable. Letting go, she stood back and tried to read what she could in his expression.

He worried over something.

"We did not expect you," she said.

"Your sister said as much," he said, his voice stiff, as always.

"But of course, you are always welcome."

Gillian frowned. She clearly didn't agree with the sentiment. Allie knew her sister hadn't forgiven their father after the business with Covington. She herself saw things differently. The man, though he had made plenty of mistakes, was still their father.

He inclined his head to Allie, acknowledging her remark.

"I was telling your sister . . . I must speak to de Sowlis immediately on an important matter."

"And," Gillian said, her voice dripping with disappointment, "I had just finished explaining that he was welcome to share that important matter with me."

Allie looked back and forth between them. This was a years-old struggle that had followed them from the secluded wilds of northeast England to Highgate End. It was as if they'd never left Lyndwood. Now that the guests were all gone, the great hall almost felt as eerily quiet as their childhood home.

Her maid walked toward the hall's entrance, where they stood across from one another.

"Morgan could show you to—"

"There is no time," he said. "I must speak to—"

"Me?" Graeme walked up beside his wife, extending his hand to their father in greeting. "Lyndwood."

"De Sowlis."

Graeme hid his contempt well. It was a known fact he hated their father for having used Gillian, and later her, as a pawn to pay off the debts necessary to keep their ancestral home.

"You can speak freely in front of your daughter."

Father clearly did not agree. Nor would he ever share important news with a woman. Though Graeme and Gillian handled the affairs of Highgate End together, such was not the case with her own parents.

"Gillian," she said, "why don't we—"

"Nay," her sister said, her eyes flashing. Allie did not take offense. It was odd, their role reversal. Before Graeme, Gillian would never have thought to disobey their father. Now she held her chin high and would not budge.

Rather than acknowledge Gillian, their father turned squarely toward Graeme. "Caxton cannot be trusted."

Graeme folded his arms. "None of us believed otherwise. As you may know, we've spent the past—"

"He was behind the attack on Kerr land. He plans to raid again, this time to instigate MacDuff."

They all stared at him, aghast. The very idea was absurd.

"We do not trust Caxton," Graeme stated calmly, "but that he, the Lord Warden, would be responsible for—"

Her father was becoming impatient. "I would not have trusted this information with anyone else," he said. "Which is why I came here to deliver the message in person. As unlikely as it may seem, Caxton is not just allowing blackmail and undermining the Day of Truce. He is actively antagonizing the border clans in hopes they will retaliate."

"How do you know this?" Gillian asked.

Instead of answering her, he continued to speak to Graeme. "I would not bring false information," he said. "Not when it would put my daughters in jeopardy. I don't know what your council decided—"

"Douglas will appeal to the king to get rid of Caxton," Graeme said. Allie could tell by the tone of his voice he believed her father, but aside from a slight grinding of his jaw, he appeared calmer than Allie would have expected given the circumstances. "But we've agreed to allow March Law to remain in effect on this side of the border for now."

The implications of this information were far-reaching. This news would mitigate some of what had been decided here this week.

"Come," Graeme said, walking into the hall. "You've been traveling and will need refreshment."

But instead of following him, her father turned toward her. "I will be along," he said. "First, I must speak to my daughter."

She knew that tone. That face. He'd used both to get her to agree to wed an old man in place of her sister, as if her permission was needed. And that was when Allie knew. The information about Caxton was not the only reason her father had made this trip to Scotland. And when she stepped to the side of the hall with him, Allie could easily discern his expression.

"Nay, Father, I will not—"

"I'll not ask you to marry again without your permission. But an Englishman—"

"You have Lyndwood, and both Gillian and I escaped the life you planned for us." She would not be persuaded by him. Not any longer. And though her fingers began to tremble slightly, Allie clenched them together. "My home is here now. In Scotland."

Her father's eyes narrowed. "We will speak more on this later."

It would have been so easy to agree, to pacify him and flee. Instead, she squared her shoulders, noticing the colors in the tapestries around her, bright and bold. Looking back into the eyes of the man who bore her, she said, "Nay, we will not."

When he blinked, Allie's voice softened. "When I return to Lyndwood, it will be as a visitor to you and Mother."

He never used the word "love," but Allie hoped her father understood now. Though she did not agree with the decisions they had made raising her and Gillian, she did love both him and her mother. Willing him to understand, Allie made one final appeal.

"On your next visit, bring Mother. I miss her."

And you. And Lyndwood. But I am staying here, in Scotland.

When Graeme walked tentatively toward them, her father did not wave him away. Instead, he nodded to her and joined her brother-in-law. It mattered not whether his nod was one of acquiescence or an acknowledgment that their conversation was not yet ended. She would not waver. Ever again.

Toren extended his legs in front of him. "Do you think it will work, the attempt to remove Caxton?"

Reid and his brother had been locked inside the solar for the last hour. The solar provided more light than most rooms at Brockburg, and his brother spent much time in here. It was the ideal place for Reid to recount his time at Highgate. Which he did, with one notable exception . . .

He shook his head. "Nay, I do not. But what alternative do we have?"

"I don't like it."

Reid could have predicted his brother's response. Though tolerant and more cautious than most, Toren was still angry about the attack and even more so about Caxton's appointment.

"None of us do, but the alternative . . ."

The alternative to peace was war. And though perhaps it was inevitable, both of them remembered their father's stories about life in the borderlands before the Day of Truce.

Toren sighed.

Reid understood his frustration, but there was nothing to be done. For now.

"Alex was there."

Toren sat up straighter in his chair. "Why?"

Reid frowned. "To ensure his baby brother was representing Clan Kerr well?"

"He would not—"

"He would, and you know it as well as I do. Alex has had as difficult an adjustment to Dunmure as you've had to life without him in Brockburg."

Toren simply looked at him, holding his gaze, and Reid grew restless under his scrutiny. None quite had the ability to set him on edge like his brothers did. And perhaps Catrina, whose lectures were frequent and varied and very often centered around the female company he'd once kept, but no longer. She claimed to speak so to him out of love, but Reid was certain his own mother would not have taken her role as savior as seriously as his sister.

Even so, he missed her.

"My adjustment need not be so difficult. If only you'd agree to let me start the proceedings for naming you as my second."

He sat forward and braced his hands on his knees. "Is that what you want, brother?"

Toren startled. "Of course."

Despite what he'd said to Gillian, Reid tried one last time to warn his brother away. "I am no Alex."

Toren could not hide his surprise. He'd begged Reid dozens of times to allow him to put his name before the elders. He'd even appealed in their father's name. But it had all been for naught.

Until now.

"No," he agreed. "You are not."

Reid clenched his fists.

"You are temperamental and rash. Your predilection to agree to any challenge is worrisome, and you speak without thinking more often than not."

Toren's words were true, but they stung nonetheless.

"I defy any man to lay claim that he is without faults."

"You did not let me finish," Toren said. He leaned forward, so close that Reid could have touched him if he so desired. "My answer is yes. For you are also a man more loyal than any other and one who would risk himself for others, even if not expected to do so. I would be proud to have you by my side. As your chief . . . and your brother."

Could he live up to such an honor?

He thought of Allie. Her smiling face, her bravery and indomitable spirit. That such a woman could love him, want to spend her life with him.

"Notify the elders."

Toren jumped from his seat and pulled Reid up with him. He embraced him, clasping him so hard it would have hurt had they not been of equal height and build.

"Why now?" Toren finally asked, stepping back.

Wanting to get it over with, Reid admitted, "I am in love."

He braced himself for his brother's reaction. To his own ears, he sounded like a fool. And clearly Toren could not have been more surprised.

"Pardon?" He sat back down as if the words had affected his ability to stand.

"I am in love," he repeated. "And would bring my future wife to Brockburg as the wife of Clan Kerr's tanist." The words came more easily now. The idea of him serving in such a position felt much less absurd than it had before Highgate. And though he was not Alex, he did not need to be his brother. He needed only to be the man Allie looked at with reverence in her eyes.

"I see."

"She is the sister of Lady Gillian Bowman, wife of—"

"Graeme de Sowlis," Toren finished.

Reid waited and was quickly rewarded.

Toren's smile was no less irritating than he'd expected. "An Englishwoman? Are there not enough Scots women for you to choose from?"

They were the exact words he'd spoken to Toren when his brother had returned from England with Juliette.

Reid rolled his eyes.

"A fair English rose . . . will she wither here in the harsh north?" Toren continued to taunt.

"Enough," he said, without passion.

"And so, the end of my brother as I know him. From the training yard to a lover's knee, bent before his—"

"Enough!"

Though Reid's was voice raised, his ire was not. In fact, he almost enjoyed the teasing, as if his impending marriage were real. Until she was here, by his side, their plans for the future could still slip away like smoke through his fingers.

"Pardon, my lords."

Their steward stood at the entrance to the solar, his stricken expression completely eradicating Reid's smile.

"There's been another attack. Your attention—"

He did not finish before Toren and Reid were out of their seats and into the corridor. The man hurried along with them, relating details about the attack just across on the southernmost edge of Kerr land. A farmer and his wife had been severely injured attempting to lay claim to what was rightfully his, even if the English reivers attempted to say otherwise about the cattle they'd stolen. Reid thought of Douglas, who'd likely already reached Edinburgh, and of the pact they had just made. He could see the chiefs' resolute expressions as they agreed to attempt one last chance at peace.

And he knew, as sure as he could be about anything that involved the shared resolve of clans who warred as often with themselves as they did with the English, this time was different.

This time there would be no waiting. No additional chances. The confidence of the border chiefs had already been shaken to its core.

This time peace was not in jeopardy. It was over.

This time meant war.

2 2

___

"**W**hoa . . . enough."

Panting, Allie let her sword fall to the side.

"Sorry," she mumbled to Aidan, aware she'd stopped listening to him. Her sword had been swinging about wildly, as if on its own accord. Shoulders hunched, she dropped it.

"Talk to me," he said, clasping her shoulder.

Aidan. Her friend, her family. When she'd asked him to resume her training, he'd immediately agreed. The prospect was the only thing that had kept her afloat after meeting with her father.

"I cannot—" She reached for the sword, but he stopped her.

"You can. And will. Allie?" He forced her to look at him. "What did your father say to you?"

"No." She shook her head.

"Allie?" he asked, his tone firmer this time. Her brother-in-law refused to be dismissed.

"He asked that I return to England with him," she mocked. "He would happily find her a wealthy husband to whom she could dutifully serve in a loveless marriage."

"But you cannot . . . Reid?"

She made a face. "Well, of course I will not be going back."

"What did he say when you told him?"

That was exactly the problem. "I haven't told him yet. I told him that I needed time to think—"

"Time? Allie, you have no time. I heard him tell Graeme that he is returning on the morrow. I don't believe he wishes to stay in Scotland any longer than necessary."

"I know," she said. "But I have to get Gillian on my side. Father will not be pleased, but he'll be even less so if she shares her opinion of Reid with him."

"Gillian may not like Reid, but I do not believe she'd prefer for you to return to England than to marry him."

When Aidan stopped and looked over her shoulder, Allie said a silent prayer their intruder was not her father.

"My lady."

"Aidan, Allie."

Gillian.

She'd been too much of a coward to speak with her earlier. She knew they had to discuss her father's decree, but her father was the last thing she cared to discuss at the moment.

She turned. "What are you doing down here?"

"We must talk about the other reason Father came here."

"So you know he wishes for me to return with him?"

Gillian's mouth flattened.

"Graeme believes you and I should both return home for a visit. You would not have to stay," she rushed to explain. "But with everything that's happening—"

"You cannot mean this?"

"I do not like it either. But if Caxton is truly attempting to incite the clans, they will not need much provocation. Until Douglas has an opportunity to speak with the king—"

"Gill, no." She would not leave now. Reid would think she'd abandoned him. "Father will have me betrothed again—"

"He assured me and Graeme that he would not make a match for you without your agreement."

"My agreement?" Her high-pitched tone was one she hardly ever used with her sister. "Father has written more than one letter about his intent to marry me off to an Englishman. And you know how I feel about Reid. And father."

"And you know how I do. But," she added quickly, "as I said, Father promised not to do anything against your will. I made him. I'd never let that happen when it is my fondest wish you remain here with me. What happened with Covington—"

"Can easily happen again," she finished. "Just because Father no longer needs coin does not mean he would be happy to see both his daughters married to Scotsmen." She looked at Aidan as if to apologize, which is when she caught the glance her sister gave Aidan as well.

Ahh, Gill. That was never going to happen. I love Aidan, but as a brother.

Her sister thought what Reid had when they first met, and the knowledge of it saddened her. "Gillian, please—"

She'd never seen her sister behave so stubbornly. In the past, she'd always been able to convince Gillian to see her side. But not in this. She was bound and determined, enough so to sacrifice her own happiness. Because she knew Gillian would never have contemplated a visit to England, no matter how dangerous it was at Highgate, had she not wished to spirit Allie away from Reid. And if she thought there had been something more between her and Aidan . . . wanted her to remain here, at Highgate End . . . Her shoulders sagged.

But the knowledge left her only one choice.

She sighed. "Very well."

Allie wasn't sure who looked more surprised, Gillian or Aidan. "I will return with you, but," she emphasized, "I will not agree to any introductions."

Gillian ran to her and hugged her tight. "I am so happy," she said. Allie gave her sister an extra squeeze, not knowing when they would meet again. "You know I love you," Gillian said. "I only want you to be happy, and safe. And 'twill be good to see Mother."

"Aye," she said, letting go. "Aidan and I must finish here. Will you delay Father until I return?"

"Of course," Gillian said. "Aidan," she murmured before turning back in the direction whence she came.

Aidan crossed his arms, waiting.

"You're planning something," he said. It wasn't phrased as a question.

Allie pretended to be surprised. "Me? Planning something? Whatever could you—"

"Allie?"

She braced for his reaction and began to explain.

"If we do this," Reid said, "it will be in direct opposition to the council's decision."

He sat beside Toren in Brockburg's great hall, along with the other leaders and elders of Clan Kerr. Although they had not caught the reivers responsible for this latest attack, their clan was not the only one to have suffered such an attack. In the last two days, there had been multiple reports of cattle being stolen on the Scottish side of the border. It was an escalation that could not go unanswered.

"The council can rot in hell."

The others cheered old Edmund, one of his father's closest friends and the most respected of the elders. The man often agreed with Toren's decisions. But when he did not, all knew of it. The man was not known for his calm demeanor.

"You would have us go back to the days when Kerr allies were few?" Toren asked the white-haired farmer.

"I would have us do what is necessary to keep our clan safe."

"We've exercised our right to a Hot Trod. Unless we want war—"

The sound of mugs being pounded on the trestle tables drowned out Toren's response until he demanded that it stop. "Enough!"

Toren was not against a counter-raid, though he wished to proceed with caution. If there was a way to root out the offenders but stay within the law, he would do it.

"They leave us no choice," a voice yelled out from the crowd. Toren ignored it.

"Unless we want war, which may be inevitable, we must find the English reivers who did this and learn who is behind the attacks."

"And if they are condoned by the warden and the king is unable, or unwilling, to remove him?"

Edmund asked what all the others were thinking. Although they had no confirmation, the circumstances of the first attack had suggested that possibility. At the very least, they all doubted Caxton would give them justice.

"Then we fight," one of the elders yelled.

"And if that is exactly what Caxton wants?" Reid asked, bracing himself for the elders' ire. They were beyond exercising caution, beyond trying to interpret something so inscrutable.

"Caxton can go to hell," someone yelled as the crowd cheered.

"Toren," he said loudly enough to force everyone to listen. "We should talk more about this—"

"Talk?" Edmund yelled. "You can talk while your clan takes action."

"As you would have us do at every provocation, despite the wishes of the Lord Warden."

"Ahh," Edmund muttered with a wave of his hand as if to dismiss the idea that they all knew was true.

Realizing what Edmund had originally said, Reid could not let it go. "It is my clan too," he said. "And I—"

"Are now asking for a position you did not want before."

The room went silent at Edmund's comment.

Everyone looked at Reid as Toren spoke. "You received my appeal," he said to Edmund. "Perhaps now would be the time to act on it."

Edmund put his head down to speak to the other elders. Collectively, they held as much power as their chief, and now his future was in their hands.

"Now is not the time," Edmund said finally. "When this crisis is over—"

"You named Alex in one day," Toren said, clearly angry now.

Edmund stared at him intently, and Reid knew what the elder was thinking. He himself had thought it, said it. He was not Alex. And they would not name him today, or possibly ever. It had been a mistake to think he could change that simply because he wanted to.

Shame wrapped around him, choked him, but he did not look away. To return to Highgate as nothing more than his brother's bodyguard—

"We will eat," Toren said, breaking the silence. "And before tomorrow, we will either agree on a course of action, or I will take one myself." When he spoke in that tone, none dared to dissent.

Reid broke eye contact with his father's friend, but he'd seen something in Edmund's gaze. If he fell in line—if he agreed with the counter-raid—he would be given the position he wanted.

But Reid had never liked to make things easy.

23

"Until the day I die I will not understand how you talked me into this," Aidan said. Again.

"You've mentioned as much." Allie looked up at the bright yellow-orange torches that lit the night sky. If Highgate was so named because of its position, Brockburg was even more impressively elevated. From the valley beneath it, she was forced to tilt her head up to see its outline clearly.

Aidan was determined not to spend another night on the road, so they'd ridden well into the night with the four men he'd insisted on taking to ensure her safety. By now, her stomach rumbled and her eyes had begun to flutter shut, a dangerous proposition atop a horse. She caught herself each time and sped forward, anxious to arrive.

"Graeme will kill me," Aidan muttered beside her as they made the climb toward their destination.

"Unless I do it first," she teased. "You've said nothing else for two days."

He shook his head. "To think I'd always wished for a sister."

She laughed then, her mood light as they approached the gatehouse. Though she and Reid had only been separated for a matter of days, it felt like much, much longer since she'd last seen him. And while her stomach was jittery and her palms moist with sweat, Allie could not be happier with her latest rash decision.

She'd been denied her entire life, but no longer. She was no longer the girl who'd obeyed her father so unquestioningly. And while she loved Gillian, she would not let her sister control her decisions either. Fortunately, Aidan had sympathized with her plight. Besides, as he had said, her father's message needed to be brought to Brockburg anyway.

Why shouldn't they be the messengers?

"If it were not for your father's message—"

"You would be here anyway."

He ignored her and spoke to the guard stationed atop the gate-house wall. "Aidan, brother to Graeme, chief of Clan Scott, ally to Clan Kerr, requesting to be admitted entrance."

Allie had expected a delay, but the massive portcullis immediately began to rise. Perhaps that shouldn't have come as a surprise. The two clans had been neighbors, and fair-weather allies, for years. These men likely knew Aidan and Graeme as well as anyone, a fact that was quickly confirmed as they rode through the gate. One of the guards inquired about Graeme and another greeted Aidan as if he were an old friend. A third led them toward the stables as Allie looked around the large inner courtyard. Like Highgate, Brockburg was built in a circular pattern with buildings on all sides. The ground beneath them was cobbled, a sign of great wealth. Allie counted seven towers in addition to the great keep. It was much larger than Lyndwood, though less spread out.

Brockburg was an impressive stronghold.

"My lady?" A groom held up his hand, and she dismounted. They'd arrived well past the evening meal, and only servants scurried through the courtyard now, mostly on account of their unannounced arrival. A man approached them, and before she could see his face, Allie's heart skipped a beat at the thought it could be Reid.

"Evening," he said, coming closer. Not Reid. The man was smaller in stature, pleasing to the eye, and very clearly a man of the cloth.

"Father Simon," Aidan said, holding out his hand. "Do you make it your habit to wander the courtyard at night?" he asked. The two obviously knew each other well, and now that the man had been identified by name, she recognized him from Reid's stories about his home. He'd told her the priest had come to Brockburg years ago, and though his age was certainly not advanced, his intelligence and compassion made him beloved by all. Including Reid.

"As much, I presume, as you do arriving at such an hour with such a lovely companion at your side."

Allie curtsied to him. "Father."

He held out his arm to her, which she took immediately.

"I was returning from the hall to the chapel when I noticed your arrival." He smiled kindly at her as he answered Aidan. "What brings you to Brockburg?"

As they walked toward the great keep, Allie's bravado faltered.

"An urgent message," Aidan said from over her right shoulder. "For your chief. And I am pleased to introduce you to Lady Allie Bowman, whose father brought the message to us."

Father Simon looked curiously at her but refrained from asking why she would have been brought along, though he greeted her very graciously.

"God is with you," he said as they arrived at the main door, which was opened as they approached it. "Toren is still here, but he leaves in the morning."

She wanted to ask why but was afraid. "And Reid?"

The priest stopped, looked from Aidan to her, and seemed to understand immediately. At least, she imagined so by the way he was looking at her now. Had Reid spoken of her?

"At your service."

Her head shot toward the entrance to the keep. The very man who'd occupied her thoughts filled it with his presence. Allie was glad for Father Simon's escort and tried not to squeeze the life out of his arm.

Reid was looking at her. Not at Aidan or Father Simon. He watched her as closely as a hunter would watch his prey.

She did not look away.

And then he smiled.

"Good evening, Allie."

REID DID NOT KNOW what she was doing here, but he didn't care. When word of visitors had reached the hall, he'd garnered odd looks by immediately jumping up from his seat at the head table and making his way toward the keep's entrance. Of course it would not be her. There was no reason for it to be her. She'd made her position clear, and even if she had changed her mind, she would not travel alone to Brockburg.

And yet, he could not shake the feeling that the visitors were, indeed, from Highgate End. Which was why he was not more surprised to see her standing before him.

"Aidan," he amended, smiling gratefully at her companion. She'd not be here without him, though he assumed they were not here with Gillian or Graeme's approval.

"Come inside," he said, offering his arm to Allie.

She was truly here.

And I'm leaving.

Tomorrow he and Toren would ride south to either find the latest perpetrators, or to go to battle, or both. Pushing the thought from his mind, Reid concentrated on the woman who slipped her hand through his arm and followed him into the hall.

"Would you care for a room first—"

"A meal," Aidan interrupted. "Thank you, Reid."

He inclined his head and accommodated them, instructing the steward, who'd reached the entryway moments after he did, to have their belongings brought to East Tower.

"I'm sure you are aware it is a bit of a surprise to see you," he said to Allie.

She swallowed but did not speak, keeping her thoughts well-guarded.

"We bring a message," Aidan said as they entered the great hall. Toren and Juliette watched them approach. The meal was at its conclusion, and some had already retired for the evening. "An urgent one."

Reid noticed Aidan's expression for the first time. He had assumed they'd made the trip at Allie's request, but the urgency in Aidan's voice told him there was more to it.

"A private matter?"

Aidan nodded. "Aye, I'm afraid so."

"Very well," he said, arriving at the head table. "I am most anxious to hear it then, after you and your men eat." He addressed his brother and his wife. "Chief, Lady Juliette," he said, making his introduction more formal than was necessary, "may I present Lady Allie, daughter of John Bowman, Lord of Lyndwood. And her companion who we've all known since infancy."

Toren grinned. "No introductions are necessary," he said, standing. He moved around the table and stood in front of Aidan. "Well met, de Sowlis," he said, extending his hand.

"Kerr," Aidan responded. "'Tis good to see you again."

As the men exchanged greetings, Reid spoke to Juliette. "A seat at the head table if you please . . ."

Of course, there was little need. Juliette was always two steps ahead. She had already summoned a maid, and she quickly instructed the woman to add two seats to the table.

"Good evening," she said to Allie, her bright smile answering his unspoken question. Toren had told her about Allie already, just as he'd assumed he would. "I am very pleased to meet you, Lady Allie."

"And I you, Lady Juliette." Allie finished with a bow. She'd released his arm in their approach to the high table, much to his chagrin.

Reid nodded, hating the formalities but knowing they were necessary. Whatever her reason for being here, he'd like nothing more than to scoop Allie up into his arms, carry her from the hall, and—

"Please, come sit," Juliette said.

Allie did so with the grace of a woman who had been raised a noblewoman. But he would always see her as the spirited vixen who'd pointed a sword at his head.

Realizing everyone was staring at him, Reid walked around the table to take his seat between Juliette and Allie. Reid usually sat on the other side of Toren. Whether tonight's seating was intentional or not—he suspected not—he was glad for it.

"I do apologize for our late, unannounced arrival," Allie began.

"There is nothing for you to apologize for," Reid said. "You are always welcome here."

The smile she gave him was that of a woman who'd been reunited with the man she loved, one who loved her in return. Reid's heart skipped a beat. He could not wait to get Allie alone.

When he looked to Juliette to support his words of welcome, his sister-in-law stared at him with wide eyes.

"So tell me what brings you to Brockburg?" Juliette asked, turning her attention to their guest.

"Aidan brings a message." She left the rest unsaid.

"And we are glad you've accompanied him," Juliette said.

The impromptu meal arrived, and as Allie ate, Reid sat back in his chair and listened as she and Juliette spoke of her journey and of England. He was not surprised the women spoke so easily to one another. They had much in common, including an over-bearing father and a sheltered upbringing that had not seemed to diminish their love of life and the people around them. In fact, the two of them had already discovered some of those similarities, leaving him very much on the outside of the conversation.

It was only when Allie had finished eating that she finally addressed him.

"You are remarkably quiet."

"That is the least remarkable attribute of his this eve," Juliette mumbled.

"Is that so?" He should not encourage his sister-in-law.

Juliette smiled at him, and Reid knew he was not going to like what she had to say.

"You see," she said to Allie. "This is not a Reid I know well." Reid picked up the mug of ale in front of him, assuming he would need it. Unfortunately, Toren and Aidan's conversation had ended at that exact moment, and both of them gave Juliette their attention as well.

"Is it not?" Allie asked innocently.

"Nay, not at all." Juliette winked at him, and Reid knew he was in trouble. "This is a version of my dear brother-in-law that I have long suspected was there, but only the love of a good woman could bring it to the surface." She looked at Allie then. "By some miracle, God has seen to it that you've entered Reid's life, and I will do everything possible to ensure you stay there."

The import of her words hit everyone at once. She knew what she had said and was not prepared to take it back. In fact, she could not have declared her support for the match more publicly had she shouted the words for all to hear.

Most importantly, Allie did not appear offended. In fact, she seemed to be waiting for *his* reaction. If she wished for a declaration, he was ready to give one to her.

He raised his mug.

"To my savior," he said, not taking his eyes off Allie, "and the woman I intend to marry."

Allie led the others in a toast, raising her own goblet. They drank, and Juliette leaned over him to speak to his future wife.

"Welcome to the family."

2 4

———

*S*he knew he would come to her.

When the door opened to her bedchamber, Allie was sitting next to the fire, waiting.

After the meal, Juliette had pulled her away from the others and brought her here. She'd ensured she was comfortable, then the two had talked for a while.

Whereas Gillian had not made Reid feel welcome in their home, Juliette had immediately made her feel like family. She told her the story of how she and Toren had met at a tournament, a tale more dramatic than her own. They were so very similar, as if they'd been destined to be friends.

And now they would be sisters through marriage. And it seemed as if she would be an aunt as well, although they had not spoken of the fact that Juliette was obviously with child.

There was just one problem. She and Reid were not married, and although Allie would like nothing more than to say the words that bound them together forever, she still could not imagine doing so without Gillian present. Part of her wished for her parents to be there as well, though she doubted her father would ever agree to the union.

It seemed an impossible problem, and she stewed over it long after Juliette left the room, but all thoughts of the obstacles between them floated away when she saw him in the doorway.

Reid did not hesitate at the entrance. He closed the door behind him and reached her in just a few strides. She'd hardly finished standing when he grabbed her and brought his head down for the kind of kiss she'd dreamed about since he left. Pulling her closer, he swept his tongue inside her mouth, unapologetically unrelenting, and groaned when she responded in kind. The onslaught of sensations, from his mouth to the hard chest and body that was pushing her toward the bed, threatened to overwhelm her.

Allie could hardly stand. Nor did she wish to.

When he pushed her down on the soft feather bed, she refused to lie there alone and grabbed his tunic, taking him with her. Reid fell onto her, capturing her mouth once again. His hands were everywhere, and as she pulled on his shirt, attempting to separate it from his hose underneath, Reid found his own destination. His hand had slipped under her chemise and covered one of her breasts. As he squeezed and caressed, she finally reached her own goal. The feel of his skin beneath her fingertips . . . his back, smooth and hard, his muscles flexing as she touched him.

Then, just as abruptly as he had started, Reid stopped. He pulled his hand back and stood, looking down at her as if seeing her for the first time.

"My God, woman. I'd take you here and now."

Though she wanted to tell him to do so, the words would not form on her tongue. She'd been trained too well, and they were not yet married . . .

But she was sorely tempted.

"Could we marry tonight?" she teased, sitting up and crossing her legs under her.

Reid walked away from the bed and began to pace in the center of the chamber.

"We could," he said, turning back to her. "We've only to say the words."

He was serious. Reid watched her, waited for her response. And while no church or priest, including Father Simon, nor witnesses or even her father's consent was needed, Allie knew her answer before she opened her mouth to speak.

"I cannot," she said. "To do so would ensure the wrath of my family forever."

Reid licked his lower lip, something she wished he would not do, and began to pace again.

"A wrath I would readily accept, though I know you cannot."

Allie watched him for a moment and said, "Come. Sit with me."

His expression made her laugh.

"I will not eat you," she said. For a man so strong and powerful, he looked terrified of coming close to her.

"I will," he said, taking a deep breath. "In a moment."

Allie contented herself with watching him, amused and aroused that she had this powerful an effect on such a man. Finally, after a few more turns around the room, he approached the bed.

"Fair warning, my English maiden. My struggle to not touch you will be a hard-fought battle, and I'm likely to lose."

Chuckling, she pulled him toward her as he sat across from her on the bed. "Look, you are touching me and nothing untoward is happening."

"Yet."

They sat that way, holding hands, for longer than she would have thought comfortable. Oddly, words were not needed. She could sense his warmth, his love, without them.

"What changed your mind?" he asked finally. "I thought you had promised to give this"—he gestured between them—"time."

Allie told him of the recent events at Highgate. He already knew of her father's visit, so she explained Gillian's plan and watched his expression change from understanding to anger.

"England?"

"Aye," she said.

"Your sister would leave her husband and return to England in the midst of all this trouble to get you away from me?"

Allie wished there was another way to explain Gillian's plan, but there was not. "Of sorts."

He frowned.

"It is not just Gillian." Defending her sister, she said, "Even Juliette remarked on how different you are with me. And though I'm grateful for it . . ."

"What are you saying?"

"You should try to understand. You've admitted yourself that you can be . . ."

"An arse?"

Or worse. "Aye, just so."

Reid squeezed her hand, but he didn't object. He knew it was true as well as she did.

"Juliette tells me you are leaving on the morrow?" She'd hoped Juliette was mistaken, but she could see from his expression she was not.

"I wish it were not so—"

"But what of the information from my father? If Caxton is behind the attacks, is deliberately attempting to goad the clans . . ."

"I believe your father and am not surprised by his information. Something has felt . . . off. I could not explain it. But our clansmen are becoming too impatient. If we do nothing, again, Toren and I fear a rebellion."

"Against his leadership? Would they really act against their chief?"

He shook his head. "I don't believe so. But whether by words or deed, the men of Clan Kerr have friends, allies, in other clans. While they do not control Toren, the time for inaction has passed. A rebellion could come from other clans, Scottish reivers . . ."

So he really was leaving. Worse, he'd be in danger.

"Stay," he said. "Remain until I return. And then I will escort you to Highgate. But you will be my wife," he said. "And I do not wish for you to go back to England without me by your side."

She did not wish it either. "Aye," she agreed. "I will not let you leave again."

When he leaned forward, Allie was not worried that he may lose control. She worried more that *she* would. As his lips touched hers tenderly, her pulse raced. She understood desire. And love. And never wanted to be without it again.

Allie woke abruptly, unsure of where she was for a moment. Then she looked around at the unfamiliar surroundings and her memories fell back into place. Brockburg Castle. Reid. She laid her head back down and closed her eyes, not wanting to wake fully just yet.

He was likely gone by now. Reid had said they were to leave with the sunrise, and though there were only arrow slits in the bedchamber's outer walls, sunlight streamed through them. She raised her fingers to her lips, remembering the firm kiss Reid had given her last eve, followed by softer, more tender ones later. They'd talked well into the night, sharing stories of their childhood and the woes of being raised along the border. English, Scottish . . . it hardly mattered. Both sides of the border were dangerous, but at least Reid had been allowed to defend himself and not rely on others to keep him safe.

Of sorts.

If she'd learned anything from their discussion, it was that his relationship with his brothers was as complicated as hers with Gillian at the moment. If not more so. While he clearly loved all of his siblings, he also harbored a bit of resentment toward both of his brothers. Watching them leave with his father to fight battles he'd thought he should be a part of . . .

A rapping at the door was followed by a small voice. "My lady?"

"Come in," she called.

A girl, no older than ten and five, entered with a bowl of water and a rag. She placed both items on the table adjacent to the bed and pulled out dried herbs from a pouch hanging from her brown leather belt. She crushed them into the water, and the sweet smell of rosewood followed.

"Good morn, my lady," the girl said, watching as Allie rose from the bed. Since she shared a maid with her sister back at Highgate, she had traveled to Brockburg without escort. Besides, Morgan was more loyal to Gillian—she would have been stopped at the castle gates had she told Morgan her plans.

"I am Elise." The pretty but demure girl bobbed a curtsy. "My lady asked that I serve you while you are here?"

It was phrased as a question, to which Allie responded, "And I should be grateful for it."

Smiling, the girl moved to the bed and began to pound the pillows. Allie eagerly made her way to the washbowl and used the rag on her face and neck, eventually washing just about every spot of bare skin until the water grew cold.

"My lady says you may request a tub whenever you like," Elise said. "But she thought you might care to join her in breaking your fast this morn."

And so Allie dressed in one of three gowns she brought, much to the chagrin of Aidan, who'd carried nothing except his own person, his sword, and a few provisions Cook had provided for them. Elise braided her hair and then led her down the spiral staircase and out into the courtyard, which was brimming with activity. She glanced at the stable, unable to help herself, and Elise said, "They are long gone, my lady."

Allie would have asked how the girl knew her thoughts, but

there were few secrets at estates like Brockburg. The servants oft knew as much, and sometimes more, as anyone. Her arrival had not gone unnoticed, if the quick stares and whispers as they walked toward the keep were any indication.

"'Tis not often we receive such lovely visitors," Elise said.

"'Tis kind of you to say so."

The maid held her head high as she led the way through the doorway of the great keep. When they turned the corner, a vision in royal blue greeted them.

"There you are."

Lady Juliette's long blond hair lay in waves around her shoulders, a single gold circlet around her head the only adornment Allie could see.

"Thank you, Elise," she said by way of a dismissal.

The young maid curtsied and walked past them, moving into the hall. Allie was about to follow her when Juliette reached out a hand to stop her.

"A word before we break our fast?"

"Of course," Allie murmured, following her into a small, windowless alcove. She perched on the intricately carved bench with velvet pillows and folded her hands on her lap.

"So," Juliette said. "Did you sleep well?"

Allie tried to stop the flush that crept up her neck to her cheeks. "I did, my lady. Thank y—"

"Juliette. Or Jules. If we are to be related, there should be no formalities between us." She paused, then added, "May I speak plainly?"

Allie did not think her answer would matter much. She nodded.

"I fear I must warn you," Juliette said. "You may hear some things about your intended that will test the bond that has developed between you."

"Test?" Allie didn't understand.

Juliette shrugged. "Mayhap not. But please remember what I

said. I have never seen Reid this way before. You are good for him, and I know he will be good for you as well."

When Juliette dropped her hands and stood, Allie did the same.

"And unfortunately, you are about to learn the truth of my words this morn."

25

*I*f Reid did not get himself killed on his mission, Allie was going to kill him herself.

Juliette was not shy in telling everyone they met that Allie was to be Reid's wife, and for three days she had endured the whispers and stares of nearly every beautiful woman at Brockburg. Nay, she chided herself, not nearly. Every one. Allie was sure there was not one knight's wife or servant who had not either looked at her as if they thought her mad or as if they wished to take a knife to her throat for taking what was theirs. She'd even had a very embarrassing conversation with one of Reid's past conquests.

The situation would no doubt have brought Aidan to laughter, but her brother-in-law had already returned to Highgate, satisfied that she was safe and had been made welcome. He had promised to return for her after apprising Graeme of the latest attacks, but she'd insisted it would not be necessary. She planned to return with Reid and Juliette to make one last appeal to her sister.

Of course, that had all happened before she was exposed to the evidence of Reid's promiscuousness. Feeling the desperate need to hit something, she'd begged Juliette to find her a private place to train, and although she'd not brought her own sword, the lady of the keep had introduced her to Ansley, the armorer, who'd provided one that would serve her purposes. Now Allie stood before a poor, innocent tree making swing after swing. She'd thought it would help to take out her frustrations in such a way, but it did not. As she swung the sword, she cursed herself for being here, cursed herself for considering leaving, and most of all, cursed herself for being so indecisive.

She paused long enough to ensure the guard was still there, and sure enough, the man leaned against a distant tree, one that had not yet suffered the abuse of her sword. Juliette had insisted the man could be trusted to keep quiet, and since he was not even looking at her, Allie was inclined to agree with that assessment.

Raising the sword once again, she positioned her feet properly and made more measured movements—only the very act of using the sword reminded her of *him*. The slow, controlled swings came harder and faster until she was panting with the effort of keeping the sword in the air for so long.

"I would say you've emerged the victor."

Allie swung around at the voice. Her chest heaved with exertion. Instead of the happy reunion she'd imagined, she simply stood and stared at the man she loved. A man, it turned out, she hardly knew.

"Go away." An odd command since she currently resided in his home, but Allie said what came to mind. And what she wanted most right now was to be alone with her conflicting thoughts.

Of course, he did not listen. He sauntered toward her as casually as he had during that first training session.

"Who did you speak with?" he asked flatly.

Allie did not know where to begin. "Who? If only there was just one person here with something to say about Reid Kerr, the poor youngest brother whose life is so difficult he's had to console himself with—let me see if I can remember—the maid Anne, and of course—"

"Put down the sword, Allie."

She was not fooled by his voice. Though calm, Reid simmered inside. She knew the signs, had seen them before. But after the past few days, she was feeling reckless.

"Or what, Reid? Will you use your charms to seduce me as it seems you've done with every other woman who is not otherwise spoken for in Scotland? But wait, that hardly matters, does it? One nasty rumor that Anne was quick enough to share linked you with—"

"That is enough."

When he took another step toward her, this time Allie did not back away. Rather, she dropped the sword and spanned the remaining distance between them. "No, I do not believe it is. I've learned much these past few days. Though not all unexpected, I am left to wonder at my own judgment. If it were not for Juliette, I'd likely not even be standing here right now."

They stood toe to toe, but Allie would not be intimidated. He'd taught her how to fight, and that was exactly what she would do now.

"I should have warned you," he said.

"Warned me? About what, precisely? That you've bedded more women than I could count to until I was four summers? Or that the only people with kind words for you are either related to you or are enamored with you? Or that the elders will not honor Toren's request because they do not trust you? What is it that you would have warned me about, Reid?"

She should not have said that last thing—she knew he struggled to feel worthy of the position—but she was so angry, so hurt by what she'd learned that she could not help but lash out.

"You are angry."

"Angry? Nay, not that. What makes you think—"

His lips covered hers before she could finish the thought. And though she wanted to push against him, continue to rail at him, she also wanted to be consumed by him. Allie pulled him closer, forcing their mouths together as his tongue plunged into her. She met the thrust with one of her own, and it was only when Allie felt the rough bark of the tree behind her that she realized they'd moved.

Reid lifted her buttocks up and wrapped her legs around him. Supported by the tree and his hands, Allie pulled his head even closer, taking as much as he gave. His groans were joined by hers, and when he pressed the evidence of his need against her, she pressed right back. He ground himself into her, and Allie kept pace. Grabbing and pulling him, she also cursed him in her head for making a confusing situation even more so.

She wanted to leave and stay in equal measure. If not for a whistle in the distance, the choice of whether or not she should marry this man may have been taken from her. Allie would not have stopped him if he'd taken her maidenhead. In fact, she'd already begun to imagine what it would feel like, making love to this man that she adored, and despised, above all others.

"Reid!"

He dropped her and turned, Allie adjusting herself and watching as his brother emerged from the wood.

"Not now, brother," he growled as Toren moved closer.

"Now," Toren responded. "I've called a meeting, and your presence is requested."

It did not sound like a request.

Reid turned to her. "We are not done here."

Whether he meant their intimacies or the discussion, Allie wasn't sure. With one final glance, he followed his brother away. Her guard returned just as soon as he disappeared, leaving Allie stunned and confused.

What had just happened?

"WE FOUND THEM, punished them, and the repercussions will come."

Reid listened to the arguments of those around him in the great hall, but he remained quiet. His brother had advised him to keep rein of his anger before the elders—an easy task for his brother, who commanded their respect, but less so for him.

But it seemed to be working.

He'd endured curious glances all afternoon, but Reid would not be goaded. He listened to Toren's assessment of their brief trip across the border. They'd found the raiders, but rather than turn them in to the warden, they'd stolen their cattle back.

The change in tactics would not go unnoticed. It ensured the tentative peace negotiated at Highgate End was officially at an end, but they'd been left with no alternative.

"When they do come, we're ready," Toren said.

"But are the others?"

They had also sent word to neighboring clans, warning them of what was likely to come.

Reid stood with his brother, always. Even if he did believe they were being manipulated by the English warden. Aidan's messages from Lyndwood had confirmed his worst fears, but the news had arrived too late for them to stop what had already been put into motion.

It was the end of peace and the beginning of war.

"And when our own men are called to the Day of Truce for their crimes?"

Reid found himself thinking of Allie as Toren alleviated the fears of the same people who had encouraged them to take the offensive. It seemed he was not the only one who was torn. The elders remembered how much tougher life had been on the border before the treaty was signed.

He should have spoken to Allie before he left. He knew that, had known it then. But the words had refused to come.

Do I deserve to be forgiven?

His actions had been deplorable, as if bedding women and

pretending not to care what anyone thought of him would allow him free rein to act any way he pleased.

"Reid?" his brother demanded. "What say you?"

They'd been discussing the Day of Truce.

Apparently Toren was ready for his opinion.

"I believe—"

"We should not go."

Goddammit. It was Alex. Again. No one had summoned him—just as with the council, he'd come on his own volition.

"Brother? When did you arrive?" Toren asked.

When he felt a hand on his shoulder, Reid grasped his brother's hand in greeting despite his annoyance.

"Not long ago. I was held up speaking to a most enchanting visitor."

Allie.

Somehow that made it worse, as if Alex was undermining him at every turn.

His brother walked around him and sat next to him on the bench. The hall had been cleared, and Toren, refusing as always to sit anywhere but with the other men, sat across from them. The others, scattered about the room, all watched the most recent development with interest.

"We're overjoyed Dunmure is such a short distance away. To think, I've been graced with your presence twice in such a short while."

Alex put his arm around him. "'Tis good to see you too, Reid. Despite our last leave-taking. Although I don't believe now would be a good time to discuss that."

Toren looked back and forth between them. He'd not mentioned his falling-out with Alex, and clearly their elder brother was curious. But that would have to wait.

"You believe we should not send representation to the Day of Truce?" Toren pressed.

Alex looked at Reid as if waiting for him to answer first. When

Reid held out his hand, indicating he should talk, his brother did not hesitate.

"We should not. But of course it is not up to me. It did not take long for word to reach Dunmure about these recent events. Nor will it take long for the others to understand that everything has changed."

"And when Douglas returns?" Reid asked.

He had tried to remain silent, but he simply could not sit here silently while his brother, no longer Toren's second, expressed his opinion. If that was what it took for the elders to have faith in him . . . maybe he did not want the position. Surely the point of being a second was to help the chief make difficult decisions.

"What are you suggesting?" Edmund asked.

"I am suggesting—" He looked at Toren, who nodded his encouragement. His brother had told him often, as their father had done many, many times before, that support and agreement were not the same thing. "That we go."

Raised voices erupted all around him.

"If we do not go, it is akin to spitting in the face of all you've accomplished these past thirty years. I am not the only one who believes it is important not to allow the Day of Truce to be rendered irrelevant too soon. Which is exactly what will happen if we fail to appear."

"Do we lay down our necks for them too?" one of the men yelled. "Make it easy for them to chop off our heads."

"We send someone," Reid said, "so as not to break the truce. Give Douglas time to speak to the king, to learn of the new information regarding Caxton's actions. If Clan Kerr stays away, a fight is inevitable."

Toren frowned. By the look on his face, it appeared he sided with Alex.

"I will go."

Toren shook his head. "You will not. Anyone who goes will be immediately arrested. And with Caxton as the sitting warden, no amount of support from either side of the border will matter. You will not go."

Reid looked at Alex then and pointed his chin toward the exit. His brother understood and they excused themselves outside the room.

"I do not agree with you on this," he said, knowing it would not matter. Their chief had spoken.

"We've disagreed many times before." Alex clasped him on the shoulder. "But you are my brother, and no decision will ever come between us."

It was precisely what Reid had brought Alex out here to say.

"I love you, and Toren and Catrina, always." He could not allow for discord between them and needed his brother to understand. By Alex's smile, Reid knew he did.

After all, it was not his brother's fault that Reid was just beginning to believe he may actually deserve the position as Toren's second. And that he'd been proven wrong once again.

26

It was Juliette who helped her find him.

When Reid did not come to dinner and Alex *did*, Allie knew before being told what had happened. Juliette gave her a significant look, and at the earliest opportunity, she pulled her into the same alcove where she'd brought Allie to warn her about the whispers she'd hear. This time, she relayed the events of that afternoon's meeting with the elders. It would appear her afternoon had gone much better than Reid's.

Allie had been on her way back to the keep earlier, intent on changing from her boys' clothes, when Juliette found her. Her friend had somehow convinced her to demonstrate her ability with the longsword in the yard—in full view of others. Promising no one would taunt her, Juliette had followed her to the yard. Of course, everyone in the vicinity had stopped what they were doing to watch. Though she felt pressured to do well, Allie had reasoned with herself that it was as good a place as any for her to emerge from the shadows. By now, she was confident that her burgeoning skill would not embarrass her completely. In fact, when she took up the sword and showed Juliette some of what she'd learned, she earned applause from the small crowd that had gathered. It had both pleased her and nearly sent her running back to the keep.

She'd been eager to relay the events of the afternoon with him. After all, he was partially responsible for transforming her from a hesitant trainee to a passably good swordswoman.

Only he hadn't come.

Allie's stomach turned as she listened to Juliette's account of the meeting. Though she was still angry with him, she hated the thought of him feeling miserable. Worthless. And she hated most of all the thought of not being with him. Reid made her feel alive like no one in the world ever had. Allie was committed to him. Whether she liked it or not.

"If I take you to him," Juliette said from behind as they slipped out of the alcove, "you must promise me one thing."

Allie peered at her new friend, knowing better than to deny that she'd planned to go looking for him.

"Whatever you ask," she said and meant it.

"You will not do anything foolish."

Allie laughed. "You sound very much like my sister now."

Juliette raised a brow. "And she would be leading you to Reid's bedchamber, would she?"

"Nay! Never that," she admitted, the corners of her mouth lifting against their will.

As she fell in next to Juliette, Allie realized they were heading in the same direction as her guest room. "The east tower?"

Juliette gave her a knowing look. "You do not believe you are there by accident, do you?"

Allie hugged herself against the chilly night air. Soon it would turn from cool to cold, and her favorite season would arrive. Gillian had always found it strange that Allie preferred winter. But there was something invigorating about coming inside to a warm, roaring fire when the world outside was harsh and cold.

"I suppose not." She turned to look at Juliette as they walked.

"You are right, you know. If my sister were here, she would be walking me in the very opposite direction."

Juliette frowned. "Despite his past transgressions, my brother-in-law is a good man who has lost his way. He would make a fine husband to you. If I did not believe that, I'd never have encouraged the match. Nor, do I believe, would Aidan."

The same thought had occurred to Allie more than once.

"But I do understand your sister's opposition to him. As your older sister, I can imagine she feels quite protective."

"Quite."

They'd arrived.

"But it does not matter what I think of him, or what your sister thinks of him. What matters," Juliette said as she held out her hand for Allie to enter. Pushing the wooden door open, she stepped into the familiar entranceway. "Is how you feel."

With that, Juliette turned to leave.

"But . . . I do not know where—"

Juliette's smile was wicked. "Look no further than the chamber directly across from your own."

Allie's eyes widened. "But—"

And with a final wave, the lady of Brockburg Castle strode away.

Allie looked up the stairwell but did not move.

What matters is how you feel.

Sighing, she took the first step toward her destination.

THE ROOM WAS dark except for the faint glow of the fire, which had died out earlier. Reid had sent the maid away and let it turn to embers. He blew out the candles she'd lit and stared into the darkness.

He should have left Allie alone from the start.

She'd been talking and laughing with Juliette, so innocent and happy. Although mayhap not as innocent as when they met.

He frowned.

How could he have thought someone so honest and pure was good for him?

At first the sound was so faint he thought he'd imagined it. But when the knock grew louder, Reid knew who was on the other side. He stood and walked to the door.

"'Tis me," Allie said from the other side. "Open the door."

He placed his hand on the key still inside the lock. He could open it, pull her toward him and forget everything that happened that day. Instead, he stayed his hand and placed it on the door instead. God, she was so good.

"Reid? I know you are there."

He bowed his head and waited for her to leave.

"Will you stand behind the door, a coward, refusing to see me?"

She knew precisely how to goad him.

"I am no coward, Allie."

"Then what do you call it?"

"Love," he said, believing his own words. "I call it love," he whispered to no one. And because he loved her, he knew she deserved better.

After a moment of silence, he thought she'd left. But not his Allie. She would not be deterred so easily.

"Gillian despises you," she said, as if that would appease him. "She believes you to be a man who cares only for base pleasures and his own happiness."

He wished he could disagree.

"And Juliette thinks you are a good man who's yet to find his way. She believes we belong together."

He'd always liked that woman.

"Do you know what else she told me?"

Reid pressed his palm on the door as if he could reach through it to the other side.

"She told me that none of it mattered. That only my feelings for you are important."

His heart skipped a beat.

"And I love you, Reid. Do you hear me?"

Shaking his head, knowing he would regret it, Reid turned the key and opened the door. He stepped aside and opened it.

Her eyes implored him to love her. And he did. Which was why he had to let her go.

"You do not understand," he began, prepared to give her the speech he'd practiced all evening.

"Nay," she said, pushing her way into the room. She closed the door behind them before he could stop her. "It is you who does not understand. While you sit here brooding, I am forced to watch as you present your worst self to the world, over and over again."

He wanted to touch her. Hold her.

"I have no choice—"

"You always have a choice." She reached up and held his face in her hands. Branded by the tender touch, he was not strong enough to force her hands away. "And you are choosing to allow the pretense you've so carefully cultivated ruin everything."

"There is no pretense—"

"Aye, there is. You pretend you would rather not stand by your brother's side because you fear they will reject you. You hurl insults rather than allow yourself to be vulnerable."

"Allie—"

"Nay, Reid. 'Tis my turn to talk."

She dropped her hands but did not move away.

"I understand what it is like to be treated like a child even when you are no longer one. Or how much easier it must be to gain notice by acting out in the way you are accustomed rather than attempting to compete with your older brothers."

His hands began to shake.

"But you don't need to act that way to get attention. How do I know that? Because I fell in love with you anyway, and everyone in your family loves you as well. We all *see* you for who you are, not who you pretend to be."

He was so surprised that he could not move and instead simply stood there and stared at this slip of a woman who was telling him everything he should already know.

She reached up and brushed the single tear off his cheek.

Allie may be right, but he still did not deserve her.

Yet.

He would prove to her, to her sister, to everyone, that he was worthy. He had promised Gillian he would return to Highgate End as Toren's second, and he knew how he could gain the elders' trust.

But Allie would not like it. Toren, Alex . . . they would all be angry with him for trying.

If he told her his plan, she would be forced to lie for him, which he would not do to her. Instead, he asked her just one thing.

"Do you trust me, Allie?"

She nodded. "Aye, Reid. I trust you."

"Remember that, please."

It was time to earn the trust of his brothers and his clan.

27

"Then he asked me if I trusted him," Allie told Juliette as they attempted to decode Reid's words from last eve. No one had seen him all morning, and when it had been discovered that two clansmen loyal to him were also missing, they realized he had left.

But where? And why had he not told anyone—told her—where he was going?

"What does Toren say?"

They walked along the wall-walk, the day an unusually warm and sunny one for September. When Juliette stopped and placed her hand on her stomach, Allie froze. She'd not had any experience with childbirth, even though she'd begged her parents to be allowed to assist the midwife. But she would do whatever was necessary to help her friend when the babe decided it was time to make his or her entrance into the world.

"Is it—"

"Nay." Juliette took a deep breath. "I don't believe so."

When she resumed walking, Allie followed.

"He is furious, of course. Although he is accustomed to being angry with Reid."

"So I've noticed," Allie said. "And yet they are quite close."

Juliette chuckled. "I've always found it fascinating, the bond they share. Since my only brother is much younger, I cannot say I fully understand it. Toren and Alex act like brothers, but they've always treated Catrina and Reid differently."

"Differently?"

"As if they're their parents as much as their siblings. I've spoken to Toren about it many times, but he does not agree." She shrugged. "And I know he loves all of them very much." She gave Allie a sideways look. "You understand that if Reid becomes Toren's second—"

"*When* he does so," Allie corrected.

"Aye, when he does so, it means you will reside here, at Brockburg."

Juliette was worried. Allie could both hear it in her voice and see it in her eyes. But why?

"Aye, I've thought of that," she said, unsure how to proceed. She'd hoped Juliette would be glad to have her here. Had she been wrong?

"You understand," Allie added tentatively, "I would never presume to interfere—"

Juliette stopped. "Please never say such a thing. How could you interfere when this will be your home too? Do you know how wonderful it will be to have female companionship, someone to help run Brockburg Castle who understands that even when the world around our castle walls is crumbling, especially then, some semblance of normality must be preserved?"

Allie's chest swelled with gratitude. "I only meant—"

"I know what you meant." Juliette's firm tone did not allow for further discussion on the topic. "And we will never again discuss such matters. This will be our home, and together, we will see our clan flourish."

Our clan.

A blanket of warmth spread over her body at those two words she never imagined hearing.

"Well, I may have a clan, but I do not have a husband," she said. "Or even a betrothed."

They looked out across the vast fields, silent.

The idea came to her in a flash. "Oh no." Allie shook her head. "No, Reid—"

"What is it?"

He would not . . . could not. She would kill him! If Reid made it back alive, she would kill him.

She looked at Juliette. "I may know where he went. I fear he's gone to the Day of Truce."

How had it not occurred to her earlier? "He firmly believed that to skip the Day of Truce was the same as a declaration of war. And with no word yet from Douglas . . ."

Oh dear.

"No!" Juliette's panic-laden voice was not making her feel more at ease. "He would not. Not against the wishes of his chief. He will be taken, put on trial for the recent raid . . ."

Every word she said sent a fresh jolt of fear through Allie. It struck her that her father's warning was what had spurred him into action. Without the confirmation that Caxton was indeed attempting to goad the clans into rebellion, he may not have acted.

Allie looked out at the horizon. How had this all gone so terribly wrong?

Do you trust me?

She did. And despite the feeling that everything was crumbling around her, Allie would stay strong and trust that Reid knew what he was doing. She had no other recourse.

Please, God, keep him safe. Please, please bring Reid back to me.

THIS HAD BEEN A MISTAKE.

He'd been wrong to come. And now he would pay with his life.

Reid chided himself yet again for his foolish, rash action. How would Toren react when he saw him in chains?

No sooner had he arrived than he had been arrested for Clan Kerr's counter-raid into England. The day had already been officially underway at the time, and Reid had noticed two things.

First, Caxton himself was not in attendance. It was highly unusual for one of the wardens to fail to attend the monthly event that held the tentative peace together. It set a strange tone, as if both sides had already given up.

More importantly, Reid noted that all of the clans were represented. He spied de Sowlis in the distance, Graeme's imposing height not difficult to miss, and he was not the only chief in attendance. The clans had agreed to come, to await word from Douglas, but Reid had assumed at least some of the other leaders would make the same decision as his brother.

Little consolation now that he was being brought to trial against witnesses who'd seen him with their own eyes. Oddly, or perhaps not so, the men who'd instigated the counter-raid were not present. And neither were the ones who had attacked his brother.

The council's assessment of Caxton had been accurate. He grew bolder, his bribes bigger, and even in his absence his treachery was present.

Reid listened dispassionately as his list of crimes was read from a short distance away. It was only when the crowd parted and his brother appeared that he felt fear.

An English prison would be preferable to what he would be forced to endure now. Toren's disappointment. He'd meant to impress his brother, and Allie, but instead he'd only proven, yet again, that he could not be trusted. He'd given the elders another reason to deny his appeal.

Toren strode directly toward the sheriff, who spoke and

stopped the proceedings, and though Reid was too far away to hear what was said, he had never seen his brother look so angry. He pointed at Reid, and then across the field to where the English officers stood, and before long, each of the clan chiefs or representatives moved to stand beside him.

In Caxton's absence, his sheriff presided in his place. Reid had planned to demand the handwarcelle, a wager of battle, which could be his only chance at escaping this day. But it seemed such would not be necessary. With one wave of the sheriff's hand, Reid's chains were removed and he was roughly shoved toward his clansmen. As he approached, Toren's expression become clear.

And it was worse than he had thought.

His brother was not angry, nor did he even appear disappointed. Instead, he looked at him the way he had only once before, when Reid had first refused to accept Alex's former position.

Toren was sad. How his brother had secured his release, he did not know. Nor would he ask. Instead, Reid stood beside Toren and watched the remainder of the proceedings, unsure of what to say.

And though he should remain quiet, when it became apparent the proceedings were over, he thanked his captors loudly enough for all to hear.

"Tell Lord Caxton," he said directly to the sheriff, "the border clans will not be goaded. We are here as agreed, in good faith, despite every attempt to undermine the very process that has maintained peace since the treaty was signed."

Toren slapped him on the back to indicate they should leave after his parting words caused the beginnings of an uproar. He had disappointed everyone that day, including the one person he'd never cared to impress until now.

Himself.

28

He needed to see her.

After a hellish ride back from the border, Reid was in a foul mood. Toren was furious with him, his clansmen none the less so, and the few words they had spoken on the ride back had not been pleasant ones.

In the past, Reid would have consoled himself with a willing woman, a tavern, or both. He'd have silently railed at his brother for failing to listen to him, even if he was in the wrong. The downward spiral would have lasted for days, if not longer.

But not tonight.

After fetching a tankard of ale, Reid made his way to Allie's bedchamber. He stopped outside of her door, suddenly unsure. Would she want to let him in?

He did not deserve this woman, but neither could he stay away from her.

Reid knocked.

He waited and listened.

Nothing.

Another knock. More silence.

He'd already looked for her in the hall, so he knew she was not there.

"Allie?" he called.

With his free hand, he pushed the door open.

She was not there.

His heart skipped a beat. Had she left Brockburg? Who would have given her escort? Though the trip was mostly on either Kerr or Scott land, that no longer seemed to matter. The recent raids had been pushing north and hitting much closer to them than they had in years.

He put the tankard down on a table and left the room, practically running back down the stairwell and out into the night. He earned a few odd looks when he burst back into the hall moments after leaving it, but nothing more. Allie was nowhere to be seen.

He looked everywhere . . . the wall-walk, the kitchen, each room in the great keep. He considered stopping to ask one of the servants whether she'd left, but Reid was too afraid of the answer.

"Reid?"

He spun around to face Father Simon. The courtyard was nearly empty but for the priest. Two young girls scurried past them, their giggling echoing long after they had left.

"It appears you are not the only one awake past the time you should be."

Despite his worry for Allie, Reid stopped to answer the priest.

"And what of you, Father Simon? Lurking in the shadows as usual, I see?" Reid scanned the courtyard as if she might appear from the darkness.

"Looking for someone?"

Reid was never sure how he did it, but Father knew everything, from what to do about the flowers that failed to sprout in the spring to what decisions Toren had made. Sometimes it seemed like he knew before the chief himself.

He did not want the answer, but he asked the question anyway.

"She's gone, isn't she?"

Father Simon frowned, giving Reid an all-too-familiar look.

Reid sighed loudly and crossed his arms. "Just once save your lecture—"

"That you would ask such a question tells me you know even less than I'd expected."

"A riddle—"

"No riddle, Reid. An observation." Father Simon's lips pursed before he spoke again. "Why do you believe she is gone?"

The priest had the answer he sought, of that there was no doubt.

"Can we play after you tell me whether Allie is still here at Brockburg?"

Father Simon just stared at him, his lack of an answer enough of an answer.

"Very well." He thought about the question for a moment and then shrugged. "I know not why."

"Consider the question more carefully."

If any other man suggested such a thing, Reid would walk away. But he'd not insult Father Simon that way, even if every muscle in his body tensed and he wanted nothing more than to continue looking for Allie himself.

"I made a mistake," he said. "Going to the Day of Truce."

"And that is why you believe she left?"

In fact, no.

"Perhaps she changed her mind," he said, more hesitantly.

"About marrying you?"

"Aye," he ventured.

"And why do you believe she may have changed her mind?"

"Father, I would really like to know—"

"If Lady Allie is still here at Brockburg. I know, son. And I have your answer. But first, tell me, why do you believe she may have changed her mind?"

Reid began to think of the reasons why, but entertaining such thoughts was too painful. Instead, he answered glibly, "Because I would have if given the opportunity."

Father hated when Reid used that tone, but what else could he do? He simply wanted to know if she had gone back, and if so, with whom.

"She is in the training yard."

It felt as if his whole body relaxed at once. His relief at hearing Father's words was equal to—nay, greater than—when he'd seen Toren at the border.

"Thank you," he said, turning toward the pathway that led to the small area on the other side of the great keep. When Father Simon bade him a good night, Reid called back the same. Running now, he stopped only when the clearing came into view ahead of him. He and his men trained in a much larger area beyond the walls, so this spot was hardly used, especially at this time of night. The only light came from the torches bracketed to the walls above it.

But that did not appear to stop Allie.

She stood alone, the training sword in her hand, her movements slow and graceful. Still hidden in the shadows, Reid allowed his heart to slow and his breathing to return to normal as he watched her.

Allie handled the sword as if she'd been raised with it in her hand.

He couldn't help but think of the first time he'd seen her in her training clothes. His body had always responded to her in a way that defied logic. Of course she was beautiful, any man could see such a thing. But there was something else about her, something uniquely Allie that had drawn him from the start. The day he'd left Highgate, not knowing whether he'd ever see her again, had been the hardest day of his life. Her arrival, the brightest.

Why did he believe she had gone back to Highgate?

Because she should have.

But Allie was here, despite her good judgment, and he was

going to celebrate that fact while attempting to forget everything else that had happened that day.

REID WAS HERE.

She could not see him, not yet. But she sensed a presence and knew someone stood watching her from the opening in the clearing. For a brief moment she'd been afraid, but she had Toren's assurance that she would always be safe at Brockburg. Besides, she knew he and Reid trained their men to follow a strict code of honor.

At first, she thought to confront him, but Allie wanted to finish her practice first.

"I must admit, you are the first swordsman I've ever admired from the shadows."

She dropped the weapon and looked over her shoulder. Allie had forgotten him for a moment. How could she have done that? Each moment he'd been gone had felt like an eternity.

"I am sure there are others you've admired," she said, turning completely toward him.

"Admired, aye," he said, walking closer. "Watched the sway of their hips? Been jealous of a sword, wishing I could be so revered? Never."

He wrapped his hand around hers, squeezed it ever so briefly, and took the sword from her. Moving to the wall, he stood the sword up against it. He returned, his travel-weary clothing an indication that he had come back very recently.

"You have just returned?"

"Aye." He placed a finger under her chin and lifted her face upward. Allie would be content to stand in this very yard, without knowing the outcome of his journey, and simply stare into his eyes.

"I missed you," he said, lowering his mouth to hers. He

captured her top lip first, then quickly followed the nip by hungrily consuming her. Allie responded, meeting his tongue's thrusts with her own.

He grasped the sides of her head, guiding her, as if she needed guiding. Allie wrapped her arms around him in order to feel his flesh beneath her fingertips, needing to ensure herself he was truly there. After worrying that he might not ever return . . .

Reid moved his hands to her back, and then slid them lower. He squeezed her buttocks and pressed her against him. Allie would have gasped if she could have. The evidence of his need pressed against her, and she did not move away. Instead, she moved into him as he grinded against her hips.

Reid moved his mouth to her neck.

"I would take you here, Allie, if I could."

She lifted her head to give him greater access.

"You've no idea the pleasures that await us."

Allie thought back to her bath and disagreed. "I believe I've some idea," she said, the words difficult to form. She wanted more, craved more. Grasping at his shirt, she pulled upward until she found flesh.

"I want more," she whispered.

As his mouth found hers again, Allie's entire body felt like it had been set aflame. Her breasts pressed against his chest, his hardness continuing to taunt her, and Reid's expert tongue made standing difficult.

"I want you," she said, pulling away. "Reid, I've never wanted anything more."

He looked at her for so long she began to wonder if she'd said the wrong thing.

He opened his mouth to say something and then closed it. She knew that look, and didn't like it.

"What is it, Reid? What are you not telling me?"

He stepped back and ran a hand through his hair. "Nothing,"

he said. "But this . . . Allie . . . if you could understand how much I want to make you mine. If you could feel what I feel . . ."

Reid looked down and Allie couldn't help but let her gaze follow his. She could not see beneath his surcoat, but she didn't need to. She'd felt it, and it no longer scared her.

"I don't want to wait," she said.

Reid took a step back. "Allie . . . God, please no. Do not—"

"We will be married—"

"And if your sister does not agree? You said you could live with your parents' disapproval, but could you live with Gillian's?"

She did not hesitate this time. "Aye."

As much as she loved her sister, Allie knew she could not live without this flawed, beautiful, arrogant, fearless man by her side.

He froze. "Do you understand what you're saying?"

Allie didn't hesitate. "Aye. Do you?"

Reid swallowed, and for one awful, terrifying moment, Allie thought he'd changed his mind.

"We will be married," he said, his smile slow and sensuous, as if promising she would not regret this decision.

"We will." And nothing, or no one, would stop her.

29

Allie had never been so happy.

Last eve, the very opposite had been true, and then Reid had come home unharmed, and it had felt as if the world had opened up to her.

They would say the vows as soon as it could be arranged.

When a knock at her chamber door was followed by the sound of it opening, her first thought was of Reid. But it was Juliette who stuck her head around the door. "May I come in?"

"Of course. I was just coming down to break my fast."

Allie knew immediately something was wrong. Although it was unusual for Juliette to be here this early in the morn, it was her expression that was most worrisome.

"What is it?"

Juliette sat on the edge of the bed. She spent too long fanning out her gown and smoothing its front, her attention to the material confirming Allie's suspicions.

"Juliette—"

"A meeting has been called."

"A meeting?"

"We must talk." Juliette said, "Sit."

Allie did just that, though she'd never been overly patient, and Juliette's hesitancy to explain herself tested her resolve to remain silent.

"You've spoken to Reid since he returned?"

Allie did not even attempt to deny it. "I did."

"And what did he tell you?"

Thinking back to their conversation, Allie relayed all of what Reid had said about his leave-taking. But as she spoke, she realized there was more to his tale.

"What is this meeting about?" she asked as soon as she'd finished.

"The elders are angry with him—"

"As is his chief?" she guessed.

Juliette frowned. "Toren loves his brother."

"But he is angry with him."

"Aye," Juliette admitted. "Very much so. Toren has always encouraged differing opinions. He would never presume to believe he has every answer, but Reid has always been so . . ."

Juliette was reluctant to continue, so Allie finished for her. "Difficult."

A rueful smile was Juliette's only response.

"He disobeyed direct orders—"

"Because he feared repercussions if Clan Kerr was the only one to miss the Day of Truce. Without word from Douglas—"

"'Twas not his decision to make."

Nay, it was not. It was the clan chief's decision, and Reid knew it well.

"What will they do?"

Juliette shrugged. "I cannot begin to presume, but I thought you should know. I've made arrangements for a meal to be brought here," she said. "I thought we might want to talk—"

"You're worried."

Allie did not like Juliette's expression. What did all of this mean?

"I do not like to see Toren and Reid like this. They are brothers—"

"But Toren is also chief." Allie had learned much about the relationship between a chief and his clan from living with Graeme and Aidan. Many of the customs she'd encountered in Scotland were the same as those she'd become accustomed to growing up, but some were not. And the relationship between clan members was one of the main differences.

They were interrupted by Elise, who brought a tray of food into the chamber and placed it on the sole wooden table. Allie was not hungry, but she did not want Juliette to eat alone, so they moved to the table together. It struck her that Juliette's stomach had grown quite swollen.

Allie approached her sister warily. "You should not have come up here—"

"Because I should be in confinement instead? Aye, I've been told. Many, many times. In this, I choose to listen to my books rather than my people."

Juliette read more than anyone Allie had ever met. Her collection of books and manuscripts rivaled an abbey's.

"Does it hurt much?"

Juliette spoke of the babe, her concerns for the future with the current troubles, and by the time Allie realized they had eaten all of the food on the tray, she realized what her friend had done.

"You were distracting me," she said, smiling gratefully.

"Aye." Juliette laid her hands on her stomach. "And I did it well too."

"My ladies?"

When Elise called to them from the door, Allie's heart sank. Had the meeting been concluded already?

"Come in," Allie said.

"Pardon me, but we have visitors." She looked directly at Allie. As if . . .

"Your sister is here," she confirmed. "And is asking for you."

Allie and Juliette exchanged a glance. Part of her had been expecting this, but enough time had gone by that she had begun to hope that her sister would indeed trust her to make the right decision. And she had, though it was not the one Gillian hoped for.

"Well." Juliette stood. "It seems as if this day will bring much excitement to Brockburg."

Allie wished excitement was the word for how she felt. Dread, more like. For nothing good could come of her sister's arrival.

STARING at her hands on her lap, Allie listened to Gillian's impassioned plea, waiting for it to be over. They sat in the hall, not a very private place for this discussion, but neither did Allie want it to be. She knew what her sister came here to say, and if she was going to disparage Reid, she could do so in his own hall.

She and Juliette had passed more time than she'd realized. Servants were already beginning to prepare for the midday meal as she waited for Gillian to finish speaking.

"I asked that you not do anything rash—"

"And I intended to keep that promise."

"By convincing Aidan to take you here, alone?"

Allie swept her hands up to indicate those around them. "Alone? I am not alone, Gill."

Gillian rolled her eyes.

"I am surprised Graeme allowed you to come," she said, attempting to direct her sister to another topic. "How many men did you—"

"He didn't allow me to come alone."

"He's here?"

"Aye."

By the time she and Juliette had arrived in the hall, only Gillian remained, waiting for her.

"You should not have come—"

"Of course I should have! And would have been here sooner if not for the Day of Truce. Graeme said Clan Kerr nearly did not send representation?"

Grateful for the new topic, Allie explained all that had happened, with the exception of a few details. Namely, ones that implicated Reid as deceptive. She also failed to mention the meeting, knowing her sister would find out about it soon enough.

"Has there been word from Douglas?" Allie asked.

"Nay, and tensions are rising. I fear if there is not a resolution soon, the council will have been for naught." Gillian sighed, the pain in her eyes making Allie wish they were not at odds with each other. "I hate this," she said.

"As do I." Allie brightened. "And if you will simply give Reid your blessing—"

Gillian's scowl actually made her laugh.

"You are the fiercest of sisters," she teased.

"And you are the most stubborn—"

"Careful," Allie said. "I see the beginnings of a smile. Remember you sit in Brockburg's hall, home to the devil himself."

Poor Gillian. She really was trying, but this was one fight she would not win.

"You really do love him." Gill looked as if she had eaten rotten meat.

"I do," she answered. "Please, Gill. Give him another chance. You've seen the worst of him, now allow yourself to be open to his best. Trust that even though I am your little sister, I am no longer a child. In this, I will not be swayed."

Gillian looked up, toward the head table, and Allie followed her gaze.

"They are your husband's allies and friends. A clan of honorable men, Reid included, who will keep me safe, just as they do their lady. And Juliette . . . she is—"

"Reid, come back here."

Her sister looked toward the entrance, where Toren's voice echoed through the hall.

"Reid!"

He stopped, seemingly surprised to see them.

And he was angry. As angry as she'd ever seen him. Fists clenched at his sides, Reid had been heading toward the sideboard when he spied them sitting at a trestle table. Juliette came rushing up behind her husband, and time seemed to stop.

It had not gone well.

She stood and looked into his eyes, imploring him silently. Reid seemed to understand as he turned to Gillian and greeted her as smoothly as the most refined courtier.

"Lady Gillian," he said. "I had not realized you were here at Brockburg."

Her sister smiled tightly. "Graeme is here as well."

The news did not seem to please Reid, whose jaw flexed in anger. "Of course, you are both most welcome."

By now, Toren and Juliette had reached them. If Juliette had appeared worried that morning, she seemed even more so now. Allie's gaze darted from one of them to the next.

"The meeting did not go well?" She had not intended to ask in front of Gillian, but worry had loosed her tongue.

Reid shot a furious glance at his brother and then pursed his lips together. When he looked back at Allie, she saw something in his gaze that sent a chill through her body.

"Reid, tell me—"

"I am sorry, Allie."

"Come," she said. "We can walk." She turned to Gillian. "If you will excuse us—"

"Nay."

His voice put her instantly in mind of the old Reid, the one she'd met and did not like. Cold. Harsh.

"Stay with your sister," he said as if he were speaking to a servant. The warmth with which he usually addressed her was nowhere to be found.

"But Reid, something is wrong."

For the briefest of moments, the man she loved was there, standing before her. But the ever-so-slight softening in his eyes faded too quickly.

"It is," he agreed. "*We* are wrong."

Allie only understood the words when she noticed Gillian's expression. Unfortunately, Toren and Juliette had heard him as well, and they all looked at her with pity. She couldn't move, couldn't breathe. This could not be happening.

"I am glad you are here, my lady," Reid said to her sister. "To escort Allie back to Highgate End, where she belongs."

With that, he bowed to them both, turned, and walked from the hall. And apparently from her life.

$\mathcal{R}$eid bent over, hands on his knees, ignoring the knock on the door. Pounding, more like, and shouting too. Toren's voice. Finally, his brother stopped trying. He took a series of short breaths, hoping one would fill his chest with the air he so desperately needed.

Since his proclamation yesterday, he'd tried everything he could think of to put Allie out of his mind. He'd trained, too hard. He'd taken a long, fast ride without a destination. He'd attempted to let sleep take him.

None of it had worked.

He stood but did not move. How long he remained in that position, Reid wasn't sure. But when another knock on the door interrupted his dark thoughts, he did not ignore it. He yanked open the door and stared at his sister-in-law, unable to bring himself to tell her to go away.

Juliette looked past him into the antechamber and crossed her arms.

"You are an incorrigible arse."

Did she think he would disagree? Reid was about to ask her to leave when she pushed past him and entered the small room attached to his bedchamber. Without windows or a fire, it was dark despite that the morning sun had already risen outside.

"You turned Toren away," she said, her voice flat.

"Jules, now is not a good—"

"He is distraught."

"As well he should be." Reid was not feeling charitable.

Though Juliette was obviously angry, and there was no doubt he had given her reason to dislike him mightily right now, she looked at him with pity rather than hatred. "Do you wish to talk about it?"

"No."

But the blasted woman did not move to leave. Instead, she crossed her arms and waited.

"There is naught to discuss—"

"Except that the elders denied your request to serve Toren as his second." She brought her finger to the corner of her mouth. "And I seem to recall something else. Let me remember. Oh yes! You sent away the only woman in the world who tolerates you."

His hands shook. Balling them into fists to make them stop, he struggled to remain calm.

"As I said, there is nothing to discuss."

Juliette obviously disagreed. She walked past him, into the darkened room, and began to pace. It would appear she'd picked up the habit from his brother. Though heavy with child, Juliette seemed even fiercer than the chief.

"I disagree. So you can either speak to me about it, or I will send Toren back to plague you. And know this—neither of us will leave you alone to sulk."

"What," he growled, "do you wish to discuss?"

As soon as she left, Reid would take another long ride from Brockburg. He had no wish to see any of them just now. But first he had to get rid of Juliette. No easy task.

"He does not agree with their decision."

"It does not matter."

"Of course it matters!" If she was exasperated, he was no less so. "Toren wanted you and none other."

"Juliette, it is done. They've made their decision—"

"And until a second is chosen, nothing is final."

That was where she was wrong. They'd passed judgment on him, just as he'd thought they would, and he doubted their opinion would ever change.

"I will stand by my brother, second or not, if that is what worries you."

She paused in her pacing long enough to glare at him. "*You* are what worries me. Why did you do it? How could you have spoken to her so?"

If she had taken a dagger and stabbed him in the heart, it would have been no less painful than to hear the disappointment in her voice. Well, she wasn't the only one disappointed in him.

"She deserves better." He said it so softly that Reid wasn't sure if she heard him. But it did not matter. It was done. He had promised her sister that he would return to Highgate a different man, a respected one worthy of Allie's hand in marriage. Instead, he had disobeyed his chief and lost the support of his clan.

It would have been better for Allie had they never met.

"You are wrong, Reid."

Of course Juliette would say so. She cared for him, though Reid had done little to earn her affection, and as angry as Toren was at him, his brother would still be his brother after all of this settled. They were stuck with him.

Allie was not.

Unfortunately, it did not appear Juliette was done.

"I said you were an arse—"

"Your husband does enjoy calling me that."

"Not because you disobeyed your chief . . . not because the elders have punished you for doing so . . . but because you let her go, and that was the biggest mistake you've ever made in your life. You will regret it once you stop hating yourself so much."

With a final glare, Juliette turned and left. She did not bother to close the door, so he hastened to do so lest his brother had a mind to return.

Reid did not want to speak to him, or anyone.

<hr>

"I WILL KILL HIM."

It was a refrain Allie had heard from Graeme more times than she could count since the previous afternoon. He'd said those words almost as often as Gillian had pleaded with her to leave Brockburg. She knew she should probably capitulate—indeed, her first thought had been to leave at once, never to see Reid again. She'd gone to her room to gather her things, but something had held her back.

Not something.

Someone.

The sight of the training sword she'd received from Brockburg's armorer had put her in mind of her first training sessions with Reid. In a way, this was what he had wanted from the start. For her to give up, for Gillian to be right about him. Juliette had told them about the elders' decision, and as much as Allie knew she should continue to be angered by what Reid had said . . .

She'd reversed her decision and told Gillian she was not ready to leave. Her sister had, of course, been furious. And Graeme was no less so now that nearly a full day had passed since Reid's declaration.

"I would prefer that you do not kill him," she told her brother-in-law as he escorted her and her sister from the keep. Allie had expected to see Reid at the midday meal, but he had not come, and she'd struggled to hide her disappointment. Toren had apologized for his brother, Juliette had pleaded with her to stay a little longer, Gillian had begged her to leave, and Graeme had cursed more times than she'd heard him do since they'd met.

It was becoming difficult for her to think, and certainly she could not do it like this.

"As would I," Toren said, coming up from behind. "A word?" he asked Graeme. With a final glare her way—he agreed with Gillian that it was time to leave—he stepped away with the chief.

"Would you join me?" Juliette asked sweetly, cupping her hands around her stomach, and Gillian was clearly torn. It was obvious she wished to deny Juliette, but to do so would be impolite. After a moment, she nodded her head ever so slightly.

Juliette led them down an empty corridor, through a door Allie had never used before, and outside into one of Highgate's many gardens. This one contained more herbs than flowers. Located just outside the main keep, next to the entrance to the kitchen, it was as private a spot as any. Allie had never been to this part of the castle before.

"Lady Gillian," Juliette said as they sat on the stone benches situated in nearly every outdoor space of the castle. "Please forgive my brother-in-law—"

"Gillian, if it pleases you."

Juliette's smile was warm and genuine, as always, and Allie could tell her sister was falling under her spell as well.

"Gillian," she said, "if I were Allie's sister, it is likely I would feel as you do. But I have no sisters, as much as I've always wished for one. Instead, I have a dear sister-in-law and two brothers by marriage, one of whom I very much disliked when we first met."

Reid.

At least she had managed to surprise Gillian.

"You did?" her sister asked.

Juliette nodded. "I could not understand at first how he could be so respected as a warrior, his bravery and loyalty never in question. To me he appeared arrogant and self-serving. Until I understood him, as Allie must have done from the start. I will not defend his actions," she said to them both, "but I would be remiss if I did not at least attempt to explain. When he was rejected by the elders—"

"For a position he claimed not to want," Gillian ventured.

"Of course he wanted it," Juliette said. "But admitting as much would challenge his own belief that he is less worthy as his brothers."

"That he could be just as respected as they, if he tried," Allie added.

"I can appreciate his position," Gillian said, considering their words. "And also that my first impression of him might have been misguided."

Now Allie was genuinely surprised. It was the most magnanimous she'd been toward Reid.

"But that does not mean I wish for him to marry my sister."

"I understand," Juliette said.

Suddenly, Allie couldn't take it anymore. Everyone around them had done so much talking, back and forth, ever since the night they'd exchanged promises to each other. What was the point? If Reid truly wanted her to leave, it was over. And if not? Well, shouldn't they marry and be done with it?

It was time to shove her pride aside.

Allie turned to Juliette. "Where is he?"

"I spoke to him earlier in his chamber," she said. "And he is being as stubborn as always."

"I will go to him. This must be decided today."

She shifted her gaze to her sister's horrified expression.

"He may not be the man you would have chosen for me," she said gently. "But he is the one I choose. If he will not see me, then the decision is taken from me. But if he will"—she took a deep breath, knowing what this might mean for her relationship with her sister—"then we will become husband and wife."

"But, Allie—"

"I love you, Gill," she said, "but I will not be swayed. Not in this."

When she turned to leave, Allie closed her eyes, paused for a moment, and then walked away. Every step she took was lighter than the last. Whatever the outcome, Allie had made a decision on her own, for herself, and she would not apologize for it.

She was no longer defined by her roles as Gillian's sister or Lyndwood's daughter.

She was a woman who would not be denied. Not by her father, nor her mother. Not even by Gillian.

And not, if she could help it, by Reid.

31

*R*eid jumped from his mount and began the climb toward the gatehouse. As ever, his thoughts turned to Allie. She was likely home by now, safe inside the walls of Highgate End as Graeme prepared for the possibility of battle. As he reached the gatehouse, he lifted his arm in greeting and was admitted.

He'd shirked his duty for nearly a full day now, so Reid made his way directly to the stables with the intention of heading toward the training yard. The men still needed training. His brother, guidance.

Nothing had changed, really.

Nay, that was not true. *He* had changed.

And she had changed him.

She'd made him desire the elders' respect, his brothers' respect, but they did not trust him. Their mistrust hurt. Weighed on him even now, though not as much as the knowledge that he had sent away the one person who believed in him.

"Your brother has been looking for you."

Reid handed the reins to a groom and greeted Father Simon.

"Good day, Father." No doubt he had something to say about Reid's behavior of late, some bit of censure Reid was in no mood to hear. He clenched his teeth and added, "If you are going to lecture me, then do so and be done with it."

"Lecture? Have you known me to do such a thing?" the priest teased. Then, perhaps noticing the look in Reid's eyes, he added, "No lecture today, but I pray that you will act before it is too late."

With those ominous words, Father Simon began to walk away, leaving Reid to wonder what he meant by that. Too late? For what?

Wasn't it already too late?

Reid was about to let the comment go, but curiosity took hold and would not release him. Following the priest, who walked in the opposite direction of the training yard, he called out, "Too late for what?"

Father Simon stopped. He looked toward the gatehouse, where Reid had just entered, and then back at him.

"I spoke of Lady Allie."

Reid froze.

"She's back at Highgate," he said, confused.

She was not. Reid could sense his mistake from Father Simon's confused expression. But he kept looking just beyond the gatehouse as if . . .

"Did she just leave?"

Father Simon frowned. "I am surprised you did not see her on your return."

Could it be true? If she'd just left, that meant she had not gone back the day before. She'd actually stayed after he so viciously shut her out. Why?

For you, you arse.

Nay, he was not just an arse. The most ignorant bloody fool in the entire country.

Despite everything, she'd stayed. She'd likely waited for him earlier in the day. Maybe she'd even attempted to find him and speak with him while he was gallivanting about, foolishly attempting to distract himself.

Father Simon was right. It likely was too late, but damned if he would let her go, again, without finding out for himself.

32

Allie let the steady gait of her horse lull her into a daze, the landscape a blurry backdrop.

Her knock on Reid's door had gone unanswered. He was gone, and no one knew where, let alone when he would return. Allie had been left in a fit of confusion. What was she to do? Succumb to her sister's pleas? Or should she follow her heart, which told her to accept Juliette's offer to stay and fight for the man she loved. The man who loved her, but not himself.

Ultimately, she'd felt she had little choice but to leave. If he would not fight for her, for himself, then she could not do the fighting for both of them.

She supposed the notion of marrying for love was a fool's quest. Gillian and Graeme did, indeed, love each other, but their marriage had been forced upon them, albeit by circumstances of their own making. Juliette . . . Sara . . . they were not the norm. A more typical marriage was that of her parents, two people who had come together at the behest of their families. Even so . . .

Allie's sigh earned her a glance from her sister, who was riding next to her.

"I am sorry," she said, not for the first time. "I want you to be *happy*. I did not want this."

"I know you did not," Allie said, though in truth she could not help wishing she were alone. She had no wish to talk with Gillian, or anyone.

Her sister must have sensed as much because she remained quiet long enough for Allie to remember every encounter she'd had with Reid. She smiled ruefully. Gillian's opinion of him had been well-deserved in many ways.

"A smile?" Gillian prompted.

"I was thinking how unlucky it was that you kept witnessing Reid at his worst."

"Unlucky . . . perhaps."

They slowed as the men in front of them came to a stop. When Allie heard the trickle of water above the sound of leaves rustling in the wind, she understood why they had stopped. Following Graeme's lead, Allie and Gillian dismounted and led their horses toward the small stream that ran across their path. Pain knifed into her. Allie remembered this same stream from her trip to Brockburg. Then, she had been filled with hope for her future. Now, the future seemed so drab. So dull. So empty of Reid.

Gillian handed her reins to Graeme's squire, who reached up for Allie's next. She handed them over and joined her sister at the edge of the stream. When she placed her fingers in the shallow stream, she jolted back from the cold. How Reid could think to bathe in such frigid waters . . .

Reid.

Would there come a time when she was not reminded of him at every turn?

Like now, as the sound of approaching riders demanded the attention of their men, Allie of course imagined it was him. Still bent down at the edge of the water, she picked up a pebble and tossed it into the water, watching as it sunk to the bottom, which was not so far below the surface. Good thing, as they would be crossing as soon as the horses were rested.

From the sounds behind her, Allie could tell the newcomers were friends, not foes, as would be expected this close to Brockburg Castle. She stood and turned, curious.

Nay. It could not be.

IF GRAEME and Gillian's expressions were indicative of Allie's mood, he would be lucky for the chance to speak with her. They glared at him with open hostility as the lady he sought bent down to the stream where their horses drank.

He ignored Graeme's questions, mesmerized by the sight of Allie picking up a rock and tossing it, the movements as graceful as when that same lady cut through the air with a sword nearly her height.

God, she was lovely. When she stood, and turned, Reid sucked in a breath.

No harsh words could hold him back, although Graeme was certainly trying. He did not intend to disrespect the chief, but Reid would not be waylaid. He would say what he had come here to say, and no one would stop him. He took one step toward her, then another, and another, until they stood face to face.

"So you finally came," she said, her voice clear and strong. Reid almost wished she would rage at him. Tell him to go away. Instead, she seemed as if she had truly given up on him.

"I would follow you anywhere, fair maid."

It took her a moment to remember that he'd said those words before. He could tell when understanding finally dawned. Her eyes widened slightly, though her expression was no friendlier than it had been that first time.

"And as I said then, I would say I'm pleased to meet you, but I do not care to perjure myself. Again."

He remembered every word of that fateful meeting.

"I told you that you would change your mind."

"And you were right. Then."

She *had* changed her mind, but he'd successfully convinced her to forsake him. Reid shot a glance over his shoulder, and as he suspected, their conversation was anything but private. While most of his men had stayed some distance away, giving him space, Graeme's did not. The chief and his wife both glowered at him.

He would do this with an audience, it seemed. So be it. "I aim to change it again. I should not have told you to leave. I'll not excuse my behavior then or"—he turned to look at Gillian, who was not hiding the fact that she was listening—"when we first met, Lady Gillian."

Reid turned back to Allie. "I thought I was doing what was best for you by sending you away." He implored her to understand. "I love you, Allie. And although you've said the same to me, I will admit that I never truly believed someone as kind as you would want to spend her life with someone like me."

"And you believe it now?"

He went to her then, her opening the miracle he'd been hoping for.

"I do," he said, tentatively taking her hands in his. "And if you will still have me, I would make you my wife. I am no one—not a chief or even a chief's second. I am neither a great lord nor a powerful earl to make you his countess. But I am a man who has learned he must earn what he wants, one who will honor his vow to love you, and only you, for every day that we are given together."

He watched as her eyes darted behind him.

"Say you will come back with me," he whispered. "Tell me you still love me, and I will spend a lifetime winning your sister to our side."

Finally, her lips turned up in the slightest smile that, to him, was the most beautiful sight in the world.

"I never stopped loving you, Reid."

He squeezed her hands, wishing he could do more, and then turned toward Gillian. With Allie's blessing, he was invincible.

"My lady," he said. "Graeme."

Both watched him, leery and unresponsive.

"I have wronged you both."

He addressed Gillian.

"You met a childish, unsure man who spent his days pretending not to care that he was the youngest brother to two of Scotland's greatest men. I promised you once that I would return to Highgate End as my brother's second . . ." The word caught in his throat, but Reid forged ahead. "And I regret that I am unable to keep that promise. But I vow, if you would give your consent, to spend every day of my life keeping your sister safe, loving her as she deserves and earning the respect that I have so carelessly tossed away."

To Graeme, he said, "You know me to be an arse, Graeme, and I will not deny I have been just that. But you also know me as an honorable man, and nothing but my death will break the vow that I give this day."

He sensed Allie had moved up behind him. And as much as he wanted to reach back and pull her toward him, Reid resisted. He owed it to her sister to allow her to react to what he'd said.

Gillian glanced at Graeme, whose slight nod was hardly discernible.

"That is a fine speech," Gillian said at last.

Reid's chest constricted. She would deny him, just as the council had. And if she did, he would overcome it, do everything possible to make her change her mind.

"But I care for only one thing," she continued. "My sister's happiness." Gillian sighed. "As I look at her face now and consider how it looked ere we left Brockburg, it is apparent I may have been wrong."

He could not wait any longer. Reid had to touch Allie, had to feel her against his skin. He reached out his hand, and when she took it, he was complete.

"I thought I knew, better than she did in fact, what would make her happy. You are not the only one who has had difficulty accepting their role." Sighing again, she shifted her gaze to Allie. "I acted as your second mother when, in truth, you needed a sister. Which I will be now." A radiant smile stretched across her face. "It is your decision to make. Do so with our blessing."

When Allie squeezed his hand, Reid finally realized what this meant. She would have him. Allie would be his wife.

Reid wanted to lift her into the air and spin her around until they both fell onto the ground, preferably one on top of the other. But he'd likely shocked his men enough already.

But Reid did not care. He didn't care about anything except Allie's answer.

First he had to ask the question. Again.

"Will you do me the honor of becoming my wife?"

Allie's smile reached her eyes, which were so full of tenderness and joy that Reid gave in to his desire. He pulled her to him, swung her about in a circle, and then kissed her as the men cheered around them. And it was only later, after they'd turned around and were riding toward their future home together, that Reid realized she had never answered his question. And so he asked again.

Thankfully, her answer was a firm, "Yes."

33

Allie could not believe how much had happened in the two days since Reid had stopped them from returning to Highgate. Though Graeme had left the previous day, forced to return home to address the border troubles, he had promised to return for the wedding. Gillian had chosen to remain, however, and it was a relief to have her sister by her side.

The banns had been posted, the tailor summoned, and all of Brockburg was preparing for another wedding. It had been two years since Toren and Juliette had wed, and everyone seemed as excited as she.

"I nearly forgot to mention," Gillian said as they strolled along the wall-walk. The sun shone down on them, a delightful respite from the previous two days of rain. "Though I do not believe they will be here in person . . ." She smiled mischievously, making Allie curious as to what she would say next. "You should receive Father's blessing more formally before the ceremony."

"More formally?"

Although Allie had fully expected to wed without any familial approval, Gillian had surprised her on their ride back to the castle. Apparently their father had announced, before returning to

England, that he would approve a match between she and Reid. Though he had "more suitable suitors in mind," no doubt all English and titled, he had admitted to her sister that he would not attempt to intervene if she was determined to go through with the match.

"A written decree should arrive any day."

Gillian appeared quite pleased with herself, but Allie still did not understand.

Only a couple of days had passed, hardly enough time for such a message to get to Lyndwood.

"But we've only just—"

"I sent the message to Lyndwood just after Father left."

Allie did not have to think hard to remember exactly how her sister had felt about Reid at the time.

"But you hated Reid then."

"And am still not fully endeared to him now—"

Allie made a face.

"As to how I could have known? You forget, dear sister, that no person alive knows you as well as I do. The only time I truly questioned whether or not you and Reid would marry was on the road back to Highgate."

"But—"

"I asked that you take a bit of time. I hoped—nay, prayed—you might change your mind. Or meet someone less . . . well . . . never mind. But I never really believed you would. And though you say Father's approval does not matter, I know how much it saddened me to have disappointed him when Graeme and I were forced to wed."

"So you asked for his written approval?"

"I did."

"Even though you had not yet given your own?"

"Exactly."

"And still don't like Reid."

"Mostly."

"I aim to change your mind." Reid had come up behind them again. He was good at that—and at making her heart beat faster with a few simple words.

"Good day, Lady Gillian," he said.

Allie turned to face him.

"And a good day to you, my fair betrothed."

Though this was the first time she'd left the castle walls since returning, she'd seen little of him these past two days. The wedding banquet was apparently a very important topic despite all that was happening at the border. Between fittings and discussions with the cook, she and Reid had seen each other only at meals, and not for long then.

"Good day," she mimicked his formal tone.

"Lady Juliette asked that I inform you both the baker has returned."

When he looked at her like that, Allie really did not give a toss about the baker. Heat rose up her neck as she remembered the dream she'd woken from this very morn. He'd given her that same look after doing some very naughty things to her.

Gillian cleared her throat. "Would you like me to find the baker? Or you can—"

"Aye," she answered before her sister could finish the thought. "I would be most grateful."

Reid bowed as Gillian walked past them. "My thanks, Lady—"

"Gillian," her sister said, not turning back. "We will be related, after all."

And while she did not seem overly excited by the prospect, neither was her tone as hostile as it had been in the past. They'd made progress, and that was what mattered.

Gillian raised her arm in parting as she walked away, the heavy material of her gown slipping upward as she pulled the hem toward her.

They watched her disappear around a corner. Then Reid turned to her.

"I've missed you," he said, his voice low and deep.

Allie made another decision.

He was to be her husband. And she, his wife. She smiled, thinking of how surprised he would be when she went to his chamber this eve in the chemise Juliette had given her for their wedding night.

She desired him, and they were to be married. Was she not the same woman the day before who had knocked a longsword out of the hands of a man Reid said was quite skilled with the longsword? Time to be bold.

"I've missed you too," she answered, no longer able to contain her smile.

She had waited long enough for the things she wanted.

No more.

REID DRANK DEEPLY from the ale he'd brought back to his chamber. Placing it on the table, he loosened the ties at the top of his shirt and sat. Stretching his legs out in front of him, he leaned back and resumed drinking.

It was late.

With no word yet from Douglas, the clan was once again split on their path forward. No new attacks had been reported, but they all knew more were coming. Caxton's plan to force the border clans into a rebellion had failed thus far, but it was only a matter of time. As long as that man was the English warden, peace was no longer an option.

Whatever happened next, Reid would do as he was told. He would accept his place in the clan and focus on his soon-to-be wife. Follow his brother and chief, silently disagree with the elders, and thank the saints he had been lucky enough to earn Allie's love.

The very thought of finally being wed to her made him hard.

He attempted to shift his thoughts. They would be wed soon enough, and he'd not dishonor her more so than he'd done already.

Bloody hell. Neither his mind nor his body would comply.

He thought he'd imagined the knock, at first. But when it became more insistent, he took a deep breath, waited a moment, and stood.

When he opened the door, he was hit with a jolt of lust so powerful his cock instantly hardened once again. It was as if thinking about her had made his betrothed appear before him.

A skill he would no doubt find useful.

3 4

"What are you doing here, Allie?"

He hadn't intended for the question to come out so harshly, but Reid wasn't sure how long he could resist her in his current state.

She didn't answer.

Instead, she entered his chamber . . . a poor idea if ever there was one . . . and lifted her chin in defiance. Did she think he truly wished for her to leave?

"I ask not because I would prefer for you to be anywhere but my bedchamber."

He took a step toward her, blood pounding through his veins.

"In fact, I sat here thinking of you, cursing my own honor and the fact that Father Simon has insisted we follow custom in this."

"You were thinking of me?"

She was as lovely as ever, her hair down, the way he liked it, and her smile sweet, but there was something different about her. He could not quite place it.

"Aye, lass. I was."

If he reached out, he could touch her. God forbid he do such a thing and attempt to keep her virginity intact for the wedding. It simply would not happen.

"What were you thinking about?"

That was it. The difference.

Allie was more confident.

"I was thinking . . ." He looked down at her bulky cloak and wondered, for the first time, why such a garment was necessary. It was drafty, aye, but it certainly wasn't *that* cold. "I was thinking of your sweet lips."

When she licked her lower lip, Reid was lost.

"And how much I will enjoy saying the vows that will bind us together for life." Lest she start to think him overly sentimental, he added, "And the feel of your legs wrapped around me."

Allie was up to something. He could sense it in her secretive smile.

But he still nearly fell to his knees when she reached up to push her cloak back over her shoulders and revealed what was beneath.

He found himself staring at a lace-trimmed, sheer chemise that skimmed her breasts.

Reminding himself to breathe, Reid looked up and immediately lost his breath again. The adventurous glint in her eyes told him Allie knew exactly what she was doing.

His soon-to-be wife was seducing him.

"If I touch you now, you will not say your vows a virgin," he said honestly. His fingers itched to touch her, to undo the dainty ties that denied him a full view of the treasure that lay beneath.

She didn't answer. Instead, Allie took the last remaining steps between them and reached for him, the implication clear.

His hands moved so quickly to the ties that Reid hardly had time to appreciate the soft fabric beneath his fingers. His mouth slammed against hers, their tongues tangling as he slid the chemise from her body and splayed his hands across her shoulders and back.

As he explored, Allie began tugging on his tunic. Finally, he pulled back for long enough to lift the offending garment over his head. He tore off his trews too, kicking them aside, and then stood blessedly naked next to the woman who would be his wife.

She laughed as he pulled her back to him. A lighthearted and joyous sound that he could not help but emulate. He was hard, ready, but Reid would not take her so quickly. Instead, he lifted her under the arms and carried her to the bed. They fell atop it together, grinning as if the world were simply perfect. Outside this chamber, it may not be. But here, with her . . .

"I love you," he whispered into her ear, using the opportunity to nip at her earlobe. Moving lower, he kissed her neck, tasting the sweetness he'd dreamed of as he made his way toward his goal. The sound she made when he took her breast fully into his mouth, tasting and kissing first one and then the other, set his blood afire.

"More," she breathed, the arch of her back telling Reid she was ready for him.

Not yet.

He lifted his head and captured her mouth once again, moving his hand downward until he finally found his goal. Ahh, so slick and ready for him. He moved his fingers slowly at first, not intending to bring her to climax just yet. But when he felt the vibrations of her moan against his mouth, Reid wanted more. He wanted her to cry out in ecstasy, and so he pressed and circled, his fingers and tongue working in tandem until he was rewarded.

She broke from him and made a sound he vowed to hear every day of his life. Reid did not relent, making sure to draw out every last syllable of pleasure.

When he did, he laughed aloud at the expression on her face. He couldn't recall ever laughing this much while making love to a woman, but she looked as amused.

"I don't believe I'll become accustomed to that," she said finally.

"I should hope not."

He waited until her body relaxed, all of the tension seeping out. When she smiled at him as if he'd given her a gift, Reid positioned himself over her.

"I want to say the words now," he said, surprising them both.

She knew what he meant, and nodded. "I'd have said them a fortnight ago."

"It will be our secret," he said conspiratorially, wondering why they'd not made it official already.

Poised over her, Reid said, "I, Reid Kerr, by the life that courses within my blood and the love that resides within my heart, take thee to be my chosen one."

Without pause, Allie repeated the words back to him.

"I, Allie Bowman, by the life that courses within my blood and the love that resides within my heart, take thee to be my chosen one."

They were wed. Some would argue an agreement of marriage and the act of making love formed the same consent as the words they spoke. But now there would be no doubt, in the absence of witnesses, to the two of them at least.

Reid guided himself toward her, ensuring she was indeed still ready for him, and prepared to make her his wife in truth.

"It will hurt," he said regrettably. "But not for long."

When he reached the barrier that proclaimed her a virgin, Reid stopped. He hated the thought of hurting her, but it was unavoidable. All he could hope to do was get the painful part over as quickly as possible. He broke through and froze, shocked when Allie wrapped her hands around his back and squeezed. She did not say a word, but her lips were pursed and she was clearly uncomfortable.

Do not look down. Do not look down.

He looked down. One glance at her full breasts and hips, curvy waist and their joining . . . ah God, why had he done it?

When she began to move, ever so slightly, Reid forced himself to wait.

"You will not break me, husband."

Husband.

Had there ever been a sweeter sound than that word on her lips?

"Maybe not, but I do not wish to hurt you anymore, lass."

He corrected himself. "Wife."

This time, her movements were more pronounced.

"Does it still hurt?"

"Nay," she said with the same smile she'd given him upon entering his chamber. "It does not."

Reid matched her movements with his own and reached up to cup one beautiful breast. "Good."

Still giving her time to adjust to having him inside her, Reid slowly began to move. Circling his hips, thrusting harder and harder, he dropped down until his body completely covered hers. He took her bottom lip, nipped it and captured her mouth in a kiss meant to devour.

He would leave her senses as overwhelmed as his own, worship her body as he did every part of her.

Reid propped himself on both hands, putting just enough space between them so Allie could watch. He looked down to where they were joined, and to his exquisite pleasure, she did the same.

His dreams of this moment paled in comparison to the sight of her under him, the feel of Allie all around him. Their gazes locked as Allie met his ever-increasing pace.

"I need—"

"You need me," he said as their bodies moved together in perfect time.

Her arms moved from his back and gripped the coverlet on either side of them. She was close.

Reid pressed himself against her one last time, reveling in the feel of her breasts against his chest for the briefest of moments, and took her lips . . . capturing her tongue and giving her every last bit of himself.

When she cried out against his lips, Reid let himself go. Together, their bodies tensed and exploded, Reid refusing to break contact as they recovered.

REID PULLED AWAY, moved to her side, and collapsed beside her. Allie wasn't sure if she could ever move again. Nor did she want to. She would be perfectly content to lie here next to . . . her husband . . . forever.

Though her body railed against the idea of moving, she did shift to her side and prop her head in her hand. Reid's smile pinched at her heart. That she could make this hardened man look so—

"You're pleased," he said. His eyes danced even as his grin deepened.

"Had you any doubt I would be?"

Reid reached up and tucked a lock of hair behind her ear. "None."

Incorrigible.

"Aye, I'm pleased," she admitted. "Are you?"

Why she should feel shy now, Allie wasn't sure. But she couldn't deny that lying beside Reid, completely unclothed, after . . . *that* . . . well, it simply wasn't a feeling to which she was accustomed.

Reid mimicked her position, but when he turned to look at her, his eyes did not rest on hers but traveled down the length of her body.

"Everything you do pleases me." He cupped her cheek and rubbed his thumb in circles on her neck. "It has since the very moment we met."

Allie thought back and challenged him. "The very moment?"

"The very one." His hand dipped lower and lay, for a moment, on her shoulder. "You talked as if Highgate belonged to you, despite the very humble clothing that had me curious from the start."

"And did it shock you to learn why I donned such attire?"

When his ministrations with his thumb moved to the sensitive spot between her neck and shoulder, Allie wondered how long their conversation would last.

"Perhaps a bit." His hand stopped moving, and the sudden seriousness of his expression startled her. "I am proud of you, lass. Your skill with the longsword has improved greatly, and I do not doubt it will continue to do so."

Allie hesitated to ruin an otherwise perfect moment, but she saw an opportunity and took it. "As I am proud of you for what you did at the Day of Truce."

"I did nothing but anger Toren and the entire clan."

"Nay." She shook her head. "That is not true. Juliette says there are others who believe as you do. That open rebellion will lead only to conflict. Especially after what my father learned."

"I should have convinced Toren and not gone against him."

Allie knew enough about chiefs and clans now to realize his words were likely true. The chief was obeyed in all things.

"Perhaps," she agreed. "But that does not make me any less proud to call you my husband." She reached up and returned his hand to her shoulder, and he immediately began to move his thumb in circles once more. She did not doubt that he loved her, and this night was proof of their commitment to each other. But the discord between Reid and his brother bothered him more than he would admit, even if news of their wedding had softened their discord.

When Reid's caresses became more insistent, she put aside all thoughts of border politics.

At least until tomorrow.

35

A week had passed since they'd said the secret vows. A week as Reid's wife. For Allie, it had been a wonderful, glorious week filled with time in the training yard and lessons on how to love, and be loved, by the man she'd chosen to spend the rest of her days with.

But for Reid, though he claimed otherwise, it had not been quite as idyllic. She knew he was troubled by his discord with Toren.

Now that Reid and Gillian were speaking, Allie's relationship with her sister had gone back to normal. She wanted nothing more than for her husband to have that same contentment with his own sibling. With the clan she knew he loved and honored.

Then, shortly before the wedding, visitors rode to Brockburg. Graeme had already returned, and was occupying most of Gillian's time, so it wasn't him. Allie and Juliette, who had been walking around the grounds, made haste to the courtyard to find who'd arrived. It was clearly becoming uncomfortable for her friend to walk, but Juliette insisted that she would not be forced to her bed before "'twas necessary." If Allie hadn't been so worried about whether or not it was safe for her, she would be amused by

Juliette's attempt to drive the poor midwife mad. The two women had very different opinions on what was best for Juliette and the babe.

As the riding party got closer, Allie counted seven men, though she could not see their faces, nor even their colors, from this distance.

"They are not English," Juliette said.

Their lack of banners had already told her as much. "You do not recognize them?"

"Not yet." Juliette stood on her toes to get a better look.

"There you are."

Reid and his brother sounded so similar, and for a moment, Allie thought it might be her husband behind her.

Trying not to appear disappointed, she greeted Toren, who slipped his arm around his wife's waist.

"Who are they?" Juliette asked.

"Can you not tell by his size?"

Two men broke away from the others, dismounted, and began to walk toward them. Indeed, one of the men was as large as Graeme.

As he approached, Juliette's eyes widened.

"Did you know he was coming?" she asked Toren.

"Who is it?" Allie asked, still not recognizing the men.

"Nay, he'd not sent word. I was warned just as we finished the midday meal. You and Allie had already left for your walk."

Allie smiled. The poor man did not know if he should concur with the midwife or Juliette.

"At least we did not get far," she offered. They'd only taken a few steps away from the keep before the newcomers made their approach.

She could see the tall man's face clearly now. And suddenly, Allie wished she did not know his identity.

"He looks quite unhappy," she whispered to Juliette.

"Always," Juliette said.

Allie resisted the urge to take a step backward.

"Lady Allie," Toren said as he approached. "Will you please tell my brother we have a visitor?"

"Of course," she hurried to answer, anxious to get away from the newcomer.

She nearly laughed at the way that sounded, as if this ferocious-looking man were here to dine with them, perhaps listen to a minstrel's tale. Nay, whoever he was, this man was here for a very specific purpose. One she hoped did not involve Reid.

"I will tell him Douglas is here."

And before she could appear rude by not greeting him, Allie turned in the direction of the training yard to find Reid.

James Douglas, Lord Warden of the Eastern Marches, was here at Brockburg.

So many questions floated through her mind, but only one truly mattered.

Was Reid's arrest the reason? Oh God, please no.

REID HANDED the broadsword to Ansley. Each day the armorer left his shop to visit the training yard to "see his weapons at work." He also maintained the weapons. He would oil Reid's sword and return it to him on the morrow. On a typical day, Reid spent most of his time out here in the yard, training himself and the men.

But today was no ordinary day.

"Where are we going?" Aidan asked.

Graeme's brother had traveled to Brockburg with him for the wedding. Reid knew he owed the man a great debt for his role in bringing him and Allie together. He'd thought of the perfect way to repay him, and it was Ansley who had helped him carry out his plan.

Reid raised his chin in question to the armorer, who nodded in return.

Good. It was ready.

"To the armory. Will you join us, Ansley?"

"Nay, my lord. 'Tis your gift to give."

Aidan shot a curious look at Reid then, but he would not reveal his purpose just yet. As they walked past the training yard, where men from Clan Kerr and Clan Scott trained side by side, Reid couldn't help but reflect, "I fear they will be using those skills in truth soon."

Aidan frowned. "They've been doing so for years."

Reid looked up as a strong wind made its way inside the castle walls. A storm was approaching. "Against reivers, aye. And in the occasional clan fight. But not against trained English armies."

They ascended a set of uncovered stone stairs spotted with moss.

"You are in good spirits, despite everything," Aidan said.

Toren was meeting with the elders that afternoon. They'd insisted on beginning the proceedings to declare the chief's second in command. His brother had wanted to wait until after the wedding, but the task had been put off too long. The clan demanded otherwise. Even Reid could admit it needed to be done. Now that they'd rejected him as a choice, another needed to be chosen.

"I am getting married to the woman I love in four days' time," he said, attempting to dismiss Aidan's concern. "War has not broken out . . ."

Aidan frowned.

"Yet." He ducked under an archway and opened the door that led to their destination. "And Lady Gillian actually smiled at me this morn."

They stood inside a large room that held every manner of weapon, some in need of repair and others freshly forged. The distinct smell made him feel oddly at home. He watched as Aidan walked through the room admiring Ansley's work.

"I had no doubt you would win her to your side . . . eventually."

"Which is the very topic I brought you here to discuss."

Aidan picked up a dirk by its studded handle and turned it around in his hand. "Lady Gillian?"

"Nay, your support with . . . Allie." He nearly said *my wife*. Trying not to smile like a young lad who'd just been given his first weapon, he pushed aside thoughts of the night they'd exchanged vows.

Aidan laid down the dirk. "I've known you for a long time."

He said no more, but it was enough. Reid would not talk about all the misdeeds Aidan had overlooked. He would no longer apologize for the man he was when he'd first met Allie. Though he still needed to make restitution for his past behavior, it was in the past. He cared more for the future now.

"You have," he agreed, moving toward the very same dirk that had attracted Aidan's attention. Picking up the one next to it, Reid handed the weapon over. The hardwood handle bore a chevron pattern and the blade itself was engraved.

"Thank you, Aidan," he said. "I bested you that day with the longsword because my will to win, and train Lady Allie, could not be matched. But I know well if it were a test of skill with that"—he nodded to the dirk—"you'd have claimed victory."

Tales of Aidan's accuracy with the blade were not exaggerated. Reid had seen him use it more than once and was glad to be the man's ally rather than his foe.

"It is yours."

Aidan looked up in confusion.

"I'd commissioned it for myself a while back. When I decided it should be yours, I asked Ansley to carve that into the blade."

"*Sero sed serio*," Aidan said aloud. "The Clan Kerr motto?"

"Aye," he explained. "Late but in earnest. To remind you that the man who married Allie is the one you championed. You will never regret doing so."

Aidan's slow smile reached his eyes. It would be easy to forget that such an affable man could be so deadly. "I never expected to."

"There you are!"

Both men turned toward the sweet sound of Allie's voice. She burst into the armory, releasing her skirts as she attempted to catch her breath. "I've been looking everywhere for you!" Seeing Aidan with him, she hastily greeted her brother-in-law, then turned back to Reid.

"Toren sent me to find you. Douglas is here."

It took Reid a moment to grasp the meaning of her words. When he did, he looked at Aidan, who was already moving past them.

"An interesting development." He lifted the dirk into the air. "Thank you, my friend."

As they followed him out of the armory, Reid took Allie's hand, fitting it into his own. Why was the warden here, at Brockburg? More importantly, what member of Clan Kerr would be greeting him as Toren's second? For as often as he'd told himself it did not matter, that he would serve his brother loyally and faithfully until the end of his days regardless, Reid could finally fully admit what he should have the moment Alex left.

He wished to be that man.

36

---

*A*llie stood. And then sat. She tapped her fingers on her knees, staring at the wall in front of her. Had she been alone in the solar, she likely would have begun pacing, but Gillian and Juliette were waiting with her.

When Allie rose to stand again, her sister rolled her eyes.

"I'm sure all is well—"

"Except that it is not."

Juliette put the book she had been reading on her lap. "What worries you most?"

As was her custom, Allie's sister-in-law spoke in soothing tones. Typically, Juliette's mere presence could improve her mood. But today was not just any day. The elders' decision had not been put off by Douglas's arrival. After Toren and Reid had an audience with the warden, they would decide on the chief's second.

Graeme and Aidan, neither a member of Clan Kerr and thus not invited to the proceedings, had stayed in the solar with the ladies for a time, but they'd quickly become restless and retreated to the training yard.

"I'm not sure," Allie admitted. "I fear that Douglas was not successful and the border clans will revolt. But I also worry for Reid—"

"He will be fine," Juliette said again. "Toren remarked just this morning how happy he has been these past few days. Whatever happens below—"

"Will set the course for years to come. Both for Clan Kerr and for my husband."

Juliette and Gillian exchanged a glance.

"Perhaps." Juliette stood, something that had become more awkward over the last few days, and clutched her stomach protectively. "I will go down and—"

"There is no need."

They'd not bothered to close the door, and the very man Allie fretted for stood in the entryway, looking directly at her. Allie could not glean anything from his expression, nor when he entered the chamber.

"Since I am already standing . . ." Juliette made for the door.

"And since we are still discussing final wedding arrangements," Gillian added, leaping out of her chair and following Juliette.

As Gillian walked past Reid, who smiled congenially at her, Allie held her breath.

"I am glad to finally see you," Gillian said. "She's been quite worried."

"All is well," he said to her sister, though he looked directly at her. "Graeme just returned from the training yard," he added. "And is on his way here."

Gillian picked up the hem of her gown. "Thank you," she said, brushing past him. The words held no malice, and when they were finally alone, she told her husband so.

"She is beginning to like you."

Reid closed the door behind him.

"Though I am glad for it"—he reached her before Allie could discern his intent—"there is only one woman whose favor I crave above all others. One"—he slipped his hand behind her back—"I think of day and night."

When he pulled her toward him and touched his lips ever so gently to hers, Allie responded by not allowing him to pull away. Though she very much wanted to know the outcome of the meeting, the feel of Reid's lips was too tempting to deny. When he slipped his tongue inside her mouth, their kiss quickly spiraled into something more. Only when Reid groaned against her and pulled back did she remember they had much to discuss.

"Well?"

She assumed he wanted to tell her something, but instead he simply stared at her.

"What happened?"

He blinked. "I love you," he said, and Allie's stomach sank. It was bad.

"I love you too," she said, resisting the urge to close her eyes against the sting of the words that were to come. "But?"

"Hmmm." He kissed her nose and stepped back, running his hands through his hair. "You assume I bring a bad report?"

The ever-so-slight upturn at the corners of his mouth was Allie's first indication that Reid was actually pleased. She had been so concerned about the outcome.

"Douglas." She shuddered. "He is . . ."

"Intimidating. Aye, lass, he can be quite so."

And then she noticed it. He was not simply pleased, he was overjoyed. Reid's step was lighter. His shoulders, relaxed. "Tell me!"

"I am Toren's second."

Her heart skipped a beat. "But—"

"Douglas reached an accord with King Alexander. He is to meet with your king to discuss the recent turmoil including Lord Caxton."

Although this was good news indeed, Allie still did not—

"He praised the clan for holding strong, for attending the Day of Truce in the face of 'Caxton's treachery.'"

"Did Toren tell him what happened?"

"He did. Which is when Douglas asked when I had become the reasonable one."

"Did someone correct him?" she teased.

"Aye, my brother was glad to do so. But he welcomed the elders into the meeting at the same time and demanded, in front of Douglas, for them to reconsider their decision. And they did."

The lump that formed in Allie's throat had nothing to do with the new promise for peace at the border. Mayhap she was a terrible person, but she could think only of Reid. The pride in his expression . . . in his very stance. How could she have missed it when he first entered the room?

Allie's eyes welled with tears as she went to him. Throwing her arms around his neck, she let those tears flow and was not even a bit surprised when she pulled back and saw a tear track down her husband's cheek. She wiped it away and kissed the spot where it had been. She kissed his lips next, a joy she'd never before known burgeoning in her belly.

"I am so proud of you." And she was. Of the man he had become, the one she knew had been there all along. The one who would serve his brother, and his clan, who would be lucky to have him. "You deserve it."

She expected his denial.

Instead, Reid simply smiled.

EPILOGUE

*I*t had been a long day.

They would normally have found lodgings for the night, the ride from Bristol Manor long enough to warrant it, but Reid pushed for the men to keep going. And as they rode up the final incline to Brockburg Castle, he marveled at the fact that he was returning home to his wife.

With his sister's babe due in the winter, Catrina had been unable to attend the wedding. He'd wanted to take Allie with him, but his visit to Bristol Manor had not been a social one. He'd apprised his brother-in-law of the ever-changing situation.

Though the latest news was good, Bryce privately agreed that war was as likely as peace.

"A meal and a bed," one of the men yelled as they approached.

"Or a woman to replace both," another said, the others laughing as they dismounted.

Once, he would have made a similarly bawdy comment, but now he only wanted Allie. He'd thought of her every moment he was away. Allie had saved him, believed in him, loved him like none other.

Ignoring the laughter of his men, Reid handed his reins to the groom and ran toward the keep. Darkness had long since fallen, and the courtyard was mostly quiet.

"Where do you run to, my lord?"

The voice was so unexpected that Reid did not believe his ears until he got close enough to the keep to see her clearly. Standing next to the entranceway, looking very much as if she were its lady, his wife smiled. His heart lurched at the sight of her.

"What are you doing out here?" He went to her, wrapping his arms around her and vowing not to let go. Not, at least, until he knew why she stood outside the keep.

"I saw you coming." She pushed against his chest and looked up at him. "Juliette had the babe this morn."

He looked up, in the direction of the master bedchamber. "Is she—"

"Well," Allie said, standing on her toes. "As is their son."

He would ask more, including the babe's name, but when Allie pressed her lips to his, he lost himself in the scent and softness that was his wife. He needed her just as he needed air to breathe. Cupping her cheeks in his hands, he took all that was offered, and more. But as the kiss deepened, she pulled away.

"Your men . . ."

Indeed, the men made their way toward him, no doubt in search of food. They'd not stopped all day except to feed and rest the horses.

"Come," she said, tugging on his hand. "You will have to wait until the morrow to see the babe. He and his mother are sleeping."

Which explained what Allie was doing in the great keep at this time of night.

"Walk with me."

Reid wound his fingers through hers and looked up to the sky.

"I could see the stars that night," he said. "When you agreed to marry me."

It was as rash a decision as he'd ever made, but the best one of his life. He had known that he wanted all of her and could never leave Highgate End and not see her again. He squeezed her hand.

"You vowed to charm my sister."

"As I've done."

She looked at him sideways. "Aye, you have."

They walked along in silence, Reid impatient to get his wife alone but also content simply to be with her here.

"She knew," he said, reminded of what Gillian had told him just before he left for Bristol. She'd known somehow that he and Allie had secretly said the vows that bound them.

"She wasn't the only one."

Reid stopped. "Who else?"

"The morning of the wedding, I overheard Aidan and Juliette. Somehow, they'd already guessed we were married."

"And from the note your father sent, I wonder if he did not surmise the same."

He had expressed his regret at not being able to travel to Brockburg, and had given Allie his blessing that she claimed not to need.

"Oh, and Aidan told me of your gift."

Reid thought of the dirk, of the alliance between Clan Scott and Clan Kerr, one that would be much needed in what promised to be troubled times ahead. "He is a good man."

Allie's grip, gentle just a moment earlier, loosened. And when her thumb pressed against his palm, the circular motion slow and very deliberate, Reid no longer wished to speak of his brother-in-law or anything that did not involve taking off every bit of clothing on Allie's body and feeling her under him.

"As are you, husband."

"Let me show you how good," he responded, remembering his promise to initiate her to a world of pleasure each and every day.

A promise he would fulfill, starting this very moment.

BECOME AN INSIDER

The best part of writing is building a relationship with readers. Become a CM Insider to receive a FREE copy of *The Ward's Bride: Border Series Prequel Novella* and a bonus chapter of *The Thief's Countess*. The CM Insider is also filled with new release information including exclusive cover reveals and giveaways with links to live videos and private Facebook groups so I can get to know my readers a bit more.

CeceliaMecca.com/Insider

ALSO BY CECELIA MECCA

The Border Series
The Ward's Bride: Prequel Novella
The Thief's Countess: Book 1
The Lord's Captive: Book 2
The Chief's Maiden: Book 3
The Scot's Secret: Book 4
The Earl's Entanglement: Book 5
The Warrior's Queen: Book 6
The Protector's Promise: Book 7
The Rogue's Redemption: Book 8
The Guardian's Favor: Book 9 (Dec. 2018)

Enchanted Falls
Falling for the Knight: A Time Travel Romance

ABOUT THE AUTHOR

Cecelia Mecca is the author of historical and paranormal romance, including the bestselling Border Series, and sometimes wishes she could be transported back in time to the days of knights and castles. Although the former English teacher's actual home is in Northeast Pennsylvania where she lives with her husband and two children, her online home can be found at CeceliaMecca.com.

She would love to hear from you.

Stay in touch:
info@ceceliamecca.com

facebook.com/ceceliamecca

twitter.com/ceceliamecca

instagram.com/ceceliamecca